Four da

A WOR

The Serpent in Eden, by Poul Anderson
The first earthpeople to explore Cleopatra make fateful contact with the eerily humanlike race of reptilians who inhabit the planet

Faber-Master, by Michael Orgill
In a time of political upheaval, a celebrated artist and his son struggle over what it means to create, to kill, to be human

Among the Mountains, by Jack Dann
A small, gentle nation becomes the seedbed of violence that threatens to engulf the entire planet

Wayside World, by George Zebrowski
One of the last survivors of the Cleopatra colony dares to dream again of an interstellar human community

---

Never before has an extraterrestrial world seemed as *real* as the planet Cleopatra, in this extraordinary work of fiction. When you finish the book, you will feel as though you have been there yourself—felt the intense "sunshine" on your skin, gazed at the fantastically sculpted mountains, suffered and rejoiced with the people of this exotic yet strangely familiar planet.

A WORLD NAMED CLEOPATRA

Poul Anderson
Jack Dann
Michael Orgill
George Zebrowski

Produced by Roger Elwood

PYRAMID BOOKS NEW YORK

A WORLD NAMED CLEOPATRA

A PYRAMID BOOK

Published by arrangement with Roger Elwood

Pyramid edition published March 1977

Library of Congress Catalog Card Number: 77-72022

Printed in the United States of America

Pyramid Books are published by Pyramid Publications (Harcourt Brace Jovanovich, Inc.). Its trademarks, consisting of the word "Pyramid" and the portrayal of a pyramid, are registered in the United States Patent Office.

Pyramid Publications
(Harcourt Brace Jovanovich, Inc.)
757 Third Avenue, New York, N.Y. 10017

Acknowledgements

A WORLD NAMED CLEOPATRA by Poul Anderson, Copyright © 1974 by Roger Elwood, reprinted from *The Many Worlds of Poul Anderson* edited by Roger Elwood, Chilton Book Co., Pa., 1974. Reprinted by permission of the author and the author's agents, Scott Meredith Literary Agency, Inc., 580 Fifth Avenue, New York, N.Y. 10036.

THE SERPENT IN EDEN by Poul Anderson, Copyright © 1973 by Roger Elwood, reprinted from *Omega* edited by Roger Elwood, Walker and Co., New York 1973. Reprinted by permission of the author and the author's agents, Scott Meredith Literary Agency, Inc., 580 Fifth Avenue, New York, N.Y. 10036.

FABER-MASTER by Michael Orgill, Copyright © 1977 by Michael Orgill. Published by permission of the author.

AMONG THE MOUNTAINS by Jack Dann, Copyright © 1977 by Jack Dann. Published by permission of the author.

WAYSIDE WORLD by George Zebrowski, Copyright © 1977 by George Zebrowski. Published by permission of the author.

"A sad spectacle (the stars). If they be inhabited, what a scope for misery and folly."

—Thomas Carlyle

DEDICATION

For Norbert Slepyan, from all the cast-
aways on Cleopatra.

CONTENTS

A WORLD NAMED CLEOPATRA

by Poul Anderson

The planetary system lies in Ursa Major, 398 light-years from Sol. This causes certain changes in the appearance of the heavens. Northerly constellations are "spread out" and most of the familiar stars in them show brighter than at Earth, though some have left the configurations because, seen from here, they now lie in a southerly direction. Fainter stars in them, invisible at Earth, have become naked-eye objects. These changes are the greater the nearer one looks toward Ursa Major. It is itself modified quite out of recognition by the untrained eye, as are the constellations closest to it. The further away one looks, around the celestial sphere, the less distortion. Southern constellations are comparatively little affected. Those near the south celestial pole of Earth, such as Octans, keep their shapes the best, though they exhibit the most shrinkage in angular size. Various of their fainter stars (as seen from Earth) are now invisible—Sol is too—but they have been replaced by others which (as seen from Earth) "originally" were northern.

Thus to a native of the Terrestrial northern hemisphere the sky seems considerably changed around the Dippers, Cassiopeia, etc. But Orion, for example, is still identifiable; and the constellations that an Australian or Argentinian is used to are not much altered.

However—the celestial hemispheres of Cleopatra are not identical with those of Earth. In fact, the Cleopatran north pole points toward Pisces, which is almost 90° from the direction of the Terrestrial axis. ("North" and "south" are defined so as to make the sun rise in the east.) There is no definite lodestar, but Pisces turns around a point in its own middle, accompanied by neighbors such as Virgo, Pegasus, and Aquarius. The south celestial pole is near Crater. The constellations that Earthmen are accustomed to seeing high in either sky are here—insofar as they are recognizable—always low, and many are only to be observed at given seasons.

Under these circumstances, it may be most convenient for colonists to redraw the star map entirely, making new constellations out of what they see. Or perhaps this will happen of itself in the course of generations.

THE SUN

The sun was named Caesar, mythology having been used up closer to home. It is of type F7, which means it is hotter and whiter than Sol. Its mass is 1.2, its total luminosity 2.05 Sol. The diameter is little greater, but spots, prominences, corona, and output of charged particles (solar wind) are fewer. It is a younger star than ours, though by less than a billion years. Either because of this, or because of variations in galactic distribution, the proportion of heavy elements in it and its planets is somewhat more than for the Solar System.

In general, the Caesarian System is a normal one. Besides asteroids, it contains eleven planets. In outward order, these have been christened Agrippa (small, hot, nearly airless); Antony (about Earth size, with an atmosphere, but not habitable by man); Cleopatra (the sole terrestroid member); Enobarbus (smaller than Earth, larger than Mars, ruddy like the latter); Pompey (a gas giant, somewhat more massive than Jupiter); four lesser giants (Lepidus, Cornelia, Calpurnia and Julia); and finally, remote Marius and Sulla (the latter really just a huge comet which has never moved into the inner system). There are two distinct asteroid belts separating Enobarbus, Pompey and Lepidus.

Seen from Cleopatra, Agrippa and Antony are morning or evening stars, though the former is usually lost in sun glare. The latter is brilliant, its iridescence often apparent to the naked eye as solar wind causes its upper atmosphere to fluoresce. Enobarbus glows red, Pompey and Lepidus tawny white. Pale-green Cornelia can occasionally be seen without instruments.

THE PLANET

Cleopatra moves around Caesar in an orbit of slight eccentricity, at an average distance of 1.24 astronomical units. Its year is 1.26 times that of Earth, about 15 months long, and the sun in its sky has only 0.87 the angular diameter of ours. Nevertheless, because of its brightness, Caesar gives Cleopatra 1.33 times the total irradiation that Earth gets. A larger proportion of this energy is in the shorter wavelengths; Caesar appears a bit more bluish white than yellowish white to human vision. The lesser apparent size is not particularly noticeable, since no prudent person looks anywhere near it without eye protection, let alone straight at it. Shadows on the ground tend to be sharper than on Earth and to have more of a blue tinge. All color values are subtly different, though one quickly gets used to this.

Theoretically, the mean temperature at a given latitude on Cleopatra should be some 20°C higher than the corresponding value for Earth. In practice, the different spectral distribution and the atmosphere and hydrosphere, modify things considerably. Cleopatra *is* warmer, and lacks polar icecaps. But then, this was true of Earth throughout most of its existence. Even at the equator, some regions are balmy rather than hot, while the latitudes comfortable to man reach further north and south than on present-day Earth. People simply avoid the furnace-like deserts found here and there.

They also take precautions against the higher level of ultraviolet light, especially in the tropics. Again, this poses no severe problem. One can safely sunbathe in the temperate zones, and do so well into the polar regions in summer. Usually there is no undue glare of light; the more extensive atmosphere (vide infra) helps in scattering and softening illumination. Winter nights are usually ornamented by fantastically bright and beautiful auroras, down to lower latitudes than is the case on Earth—in spite of Cleopatra's strong magnetic field. To be sure, solar-atmospheric interference with radio and the like can get pretty bad, especially at a peak of the sunspot cycle (for Caesar, about 14 Earth-years long, as opposed to Sol's 11). But once installed, laser transceivers aren't bothered.

Cleopatra is smaller than Earth. In terms of the latter planet, its mass is 0.528, its radius 0.78 (or 4960 km at the equator), its mean density 1.10 (or 6.1 times that of water), and its surface gravity 0.86. This last means that, for example, a human who weighed 80 kg on Earth weighs 68.5 here; he himself soon adjusts to that—though he is well advised to maintain a lifetime program of physical exercise to avoid various atrophies and circulation problems—but engineering is affected. (For instance, aircraft need less wing area but ground vehicles need more effective brakes.) An object falling through a given distance takes 1.07 times as long to do so as on Earth and gains- 0.93 the velocity; a pendulum of given length has 1.14 the period; the speed of a wave on deep water is 0.93 what it is on Earth.

Standing on a flat plain or sea, a man of normal height observes the horizon as being about 7 km off, compared to about 8 on Earth—not a terribly striking difference, especially in rugged topography or hazy weather.

Despite its lesser dimensions, Cleopatra has quite a terrestroid atmosphere. In fact, the sea level pressures on the two planets are almost identical. It is thought that this is due to the hot, dense mass of the planet outgassing more than Earth did, early in their respective histories, and to the fact that, ever since, the strong magnetic field has helped keep too many molecules from getting kicked away into space by solar and cosmic ray particles.

Air pressure drops with altitude more slowly than on Earth, because of the lower gravity. On Earth, at about 5.5 km the pressure is one-half that at sea level; but on Cleopatra, one must go up 6.35 km to find this. Not only does that moderate surface conditions, it extends life zones higher, and offers more possibilities to flyers both living and mechanical.

There having been less tidal friction acting on it through most of its existence, Cleopatra spins faster than Earth: once in 17 hr 21 m 14.8 s, or about 17.3 hr or 0.72 Earth diurnal period. Its year therefore lasts 639 of its own days, give or take a little bit because of trepidation, precession, etc.

The axial tilt is 28°, somewhat more than Earth's. However, the climate of high latitudes is not necessarily more extreme on that account. Certainly winters are less cold. It is the difference in the length of seasons—a fourth again as much—which is most important. Likewise, the seasonal variation of day and night lengths is more marked than on Earth, and the Arctic and Antarctic come nearer to the equator.

The stronger sun, which supplies more energy; the longer year, which gives more time to overcome thermal lag; the smaller size, which brings zones closer together; the larger axial tilt, which exaggerates the differences between them; the quicker spin, which generates more potent cyclonic forces; the lower pressures but the longer distance up to a stratosphere, which make for more extensive air masses moving at a given time under given conditions — all these create "livelier" weather than on Earth. Storms are more common and violent, though they tend to be short-lived. Huge thunderstorms in the river valley, twisters on the plains, hurricanes in the tropics, and blizzards near the poles are things which colonists must expect; they have to build stoutly and maintain an alert meteorological service.

But this seeming drawback has its good side. With such variability, both droughts and deluges are rare; chilly fogs don't linger; inversion layers break up before they accumulate unpleasant gases; daytime cloud patterns can be gorgeous to watch, while nights are brilliantly clear more often than not, in most areas of the planet.

Turning back to the globe itself: Its greater mean density than Earth's is due to a higher percentage of heavy elements, especially those later in the periodic table than iron. This leads to a particularly hot core which, combined with the rapid rotation, is the source of the magnetic field screening the atmosphere from solar wind. (Of course, the field is far weaker than in any generator—roughly twice as strong as Earth's—but it reaches way out.) Having not only more interior heat but a smaller volume, Cleopatra radiates more strongly.

This means that it is geologically, or planetologically, more active. There are more hot springs, geysers, volcanoes, quakes, and tsunamis, especially along the leading edges of continents and in midocean (vide infra). There is faster mountain-building, aided by the lower gravity which permits higher upheavals and steeper slopes. (The same is true of sand dunes.) Erosion proceeds more rapidly too; hence spectacularly sculptured uplands are quite common.

With the crustal plates more mobile than on Earth, we get an overall situation—there are many local exceptions, of course—about as follows. No continent is as big as Eurasia; the largest is comparable to North America. Their shelves drop sharply off to more profound depths than Terrestrial. They define—in the same rough way as on Earth—four major oceans, each surrounded by its "ring of fire" and marked down the middle by archipelagos of which numerous islands are volcanic. Elsewhere are smaller, shallower seas. Along with the tide patterns (vide infra), these factors tend to inhibit the generation of great ocean currents, and thus to somewhat isolate the latitudes from each other. That isn't all bad if "Norway" has no "Gulf Stream" to warm it, neither does the "Pacific North-west" have a "Kuroshio" to chill it, and marine life is even more varied than on Earth.

The proportion of land to water surface is slightly higher than Terrestrial, mainly because of the powerful upthrust of crustal masses—though doubtless the splitting of H_2O molecules by ultraviolet quanta, before there was a protective ozone layer, also has a good deal to do with this. However, there is no water shortage; in fact, the smaller size of individual land blocks and the vigorous air circulation make for better distribution of this substance and keep continental interiors reasonably temperate.

The abundance of heavy metals is a boon to industry, yet not altogether a blessing. Some of these elements and their compounds are poisonous to man. Concentrated in certain areas, they make the soil, or organisms living there, dangerous. But again, this is by no means the universal case, and precautions are not hard to take once people have been warned. Several beautiful minerals and gemstones appear to be unique to this planet.

SATELLITES

Cleopatra has no moon in the usual sense. Perhaps it once did, or perhaps an asteroid was captured. In any event, at some point in the fairly recent past (estimated 10 million years ago), this body (estimated mass, 0.001 that of Luna) came within the Roche limit and was pulled asunder by tidal forces.

Numerous fragments fell. The biggest left traces in the form of huge circular lakes, bays and valleys. Meteorites are still coming down as perturbation maneuvers them out of orbit. So there are many pitted rocks, many craters great and small, on Cleopatra, the newest sharply defined, the oldest blurred by erosion. On any clear night, shooting stars may be seen delightfully often.

But most of the disrupted mass formed a ring, at a mean distance of some 7500 km from the surface, which is still around and will probably last for millions of years to come. It is not like the ring(s) of Saturn, the latter consisting of tiny ice particles. Cleopatra is surrounded by a belt of stony and metallic fragments, ranging in size down to gravel and fine dust. There is considerable space between the average pair of rocks, though of course this varies.

Except for Charmian and Iras (vide infra), the satellites are too small to be seen by day against sun glare. Moreover, being nearly in the equatorial plane, the ring shows best in the tropics. In high latitudes one sees it low in the sky, often obscured by mountains, woods, or haze; and one cannot see it at all in the polar regions (above latitude 66°) aside from a few isolated, far-out particles.

The ring is at its most spectacular at equatorial midnight around the time of solstice. Then a band of hundreds of glittering, twinkling fireflies streams across the sky from west to east, the faster (nearer) overtaking the slower (further out) though all move swiftly. Irregular in shape, scoured and scored by dust, many sparkle in prismatic hues as well as white. The dust itself forms a dimly glowing background, through which stars can be seen. Though the band has no constant or definite boundaries, it averages about 10° wide, brightest at the middle, fading out toward the edges.

The mean synodic period of a particle, i.e., the time for a complete cycle from rising to rising as observed on the ground, is 7.5 hr or about 0.43 Cleopatran day. This is 48° per hr, or rather more than three times as fast as Sol or Luna crosses the Terrestrial sky. However, the ring is too close in for the entire half arc to be visible anywhere on the planet, so the maximum time observed (at the equator) is 1 hr 22 m.

That time is really only interesting as concerns the two members of the ring which are so big that they may be called tiny moons. They have, indeed, been given names, Charmian and Iras. (At the nomenclature conference, one faction wanted a Ftaatateeta but was voted down). Charmian is the larger and slightly closer. In fact, it seems just about the same size as Luna does on Earth, though its actual mean diameter is not quite 70 km. Iras has about half the linear cross section and moves a little slower. (The respective synodic periods are 7.6 and 8.2 hr, which means that Charmian overtakes Iras every 102 hr or 5.9 Cleopatran days. These figures are subject to some oscillation because of assorted gravitational influences.) The two orbits are so skewed that, while they come near, the moonlets seldom overlap.

In other words, they move along the ring approximately four times in a Cleopatran day and night, going through approximately 5.6 phase-change cycles as they do; but most of this cannot be seen from any single place on the ground.

Neither looks much like Luna. Charmian is only roughly spheroidal, Iras still less so. They show angles, facets, promontories and markings as they orbit the planet while spinning in a wobbly fashion. They both resemble Luna in being large and reflective enough to remain visible during an eclipse.

This eclipse is due to the fact that Cleopatra's shadow crosses the rings. There is sufficient axial tilt that at a solstice, only a small "bite" is taken out of the lower edge of the band at its lowest point—and the band is irregular, fluctuating, and vaguely defined enough for this not to be particularly noticeable. But as the planet moves on around its sun, the geometry changes. About 23 Cleopatran days after solstice, the shadow arc entirely bisects the ring. By equinox, ca. 160 days after solstice (ca. 115 Earth days), the eclipse is at a maximum.

At this season, when watched from the equator, the ring—including the two moons—streams upward from the west as before. But at an azimuth of about 52°, not quite 60% of the way up to the zenith, the particles blank out. They do not reappear until they are correspondingly near the eastern horizon and descending. Charmian, Iras, and a few of the largest meteoroids remain visible but turn dull coppery red from atmosphere-refracted light, as they transit the dark gap.

This cycle of eclipse and full illumination is repeated twice in the course of a year. The precise appearance of the ring, as well as its position in the heavens, depends on time and location of the observer.

But at any season—what with auroras, background skyglow, stars, ring, and the frequently seen changeable moonlets—Cleopatran nights are not unduly dark. In clear weather, a human can make his way around pretty well without artificial light.

The tidal pull of Caesar is small, about one-third that of Sol on Earth or less than one-fifth the total of what Earth gets. Were the ring particles concentrated in one mass, the total heave would be enormous, about 18 times what Luna gives to Earth. Scattered as they are, they produce only minor effects individually. But the resultants are complex and variable. The seas do not get stagnant, and crosscurrents often make them choppy.

GENERAL BIOLOGY

Given a planet this similar to Earth, it is not surprising that here too life arose, based on proteins in water solution, and in time developed photosynthesizing plants which formed and now maintain an oxynitrogen atmosphere. It *is* unusual to have so many details duplicated. (To be sure, given the vast number of worlds in the galaxy, this must happen once in a while.) Here too life uses predominantly levoamino acids and dextro sugars. Many lipids, carbohydrates, hydrocarbons, pyrroles, etc. are the same as on Earth, chlorophyl and hemoglobin included (with some minor variations). In like manner, we find viruses, bacteria, protozoa, vegetable and animal kingdoms.

Now it would be too improbable for every detail to be the same, considering how many are the consequence of random "choice" among numerous possibilities. Much Cleopatran life can be eaten by man, is nourishing and tasty; but some of it is poisonous, and all of it lacks certain vitamins and other nutrients. Hence one can live only temporarily on an exclusive diet of it. This is not a great handicap. In fact, basically it is desirable, because it works both ways. Native germs cannot function in the human body, native viruses are not equipped to take over human genetic machinery—in short, to man this is an infection-free world.

And of course he can introduce his own plants and animals. Given a start—e.g., by eradication of deadly weeds from a range—they will flourish. Soon the problem will be to save the Cleopatran ecology. Once established, Terrestrial life will spread fast and overwhelmingly unless it is controlled. For it is further evolved.

After all, Cleopatra is younger than Earth. If anything, it is surprising how far life has developed, in so much less time. Conceivably the energetic sun, the higher lever of actinic radiation and electrical discharge, promoted rapid development of the primitive protobiology and later microorganisms. But afterward, perhaps, the weak tides—making for a sharper division between sea and land—delayed the conquest of the latter.

At any rate, though inaccurate, it is helpful to think of this world as being in a "Mesozoic" era.

PLANTS

Angiosperms have not yet developed. There are primitive equivalents of the spermatophytes, including some gymnosperms. These are most common in the drier inland and upland regions. The coasts, marshes, etc. are dominated by types similar to Terrestrial bryophytes and pteridophytes, more elaborated than on present-day Earth. Because of certain root-like structures, they are known as dactylophytes.

Nothing like grass or flowers exists. Moist areas are carpeted with low, dense, intensely green vegetation resembling moss. Species of this phylum have developed protection against drying out and are therefore found elsewhere as ground cover in paler and stiffer versions. Many trees and shrubs (if one may call them that) have colorful pseudoblooms, analogous to those of our poinsettias, to lure pollinators.

Among the more picturesque plants are: The misnamed dinobryons, huge dactylophytes in wet regions which suggest spongy green many-branched coral growths; the aquatic weirplant and its land relatives, the dichtophytes, carnivorous species which grow in the form of great nets to trap sizeable prey; the Venus mirror, a bush named for its highly reflective leaves, which attract glitterwings, the chameleon plant, which exhibits changes of shade and even to some degree color, according to lighting conditions—a camouflage against eaters; thc sarissa, resembling sharp-pointed bamboo but growing in clusters which bristle almost horizontally outward, supported by roots along the stalks; the grenade, a bush whose round pods explode spectacularly, though harmlessly, to scatter seeds; the Christmas memory, a primitive evergreen whose roughly shaped but brilliant red cones are like ornaments; and the delicious sugarroot.

No one region has all kinds. Some genera are circumpolar, others not. This is likewise true in the zoological field.

ANIMALS

A biologist would vehemently deny that Cleopatra has insects, fish, amphibians, reptiles, birds, mammals, or anything else Terrestrial, other than what man may import. There are too many differences of detail, some quite fundamental. Nevertheless, resemblances are close enough—when similar environments have selected for similar characteristics—that pioneers are not inclined to split every semantic hair.

The colonists do use scientific names for the broad classes. But "worm" has so wide a meaning even on Earth that it can reasonably be applied to numerous legless invertebrates on Cleopatra. One interesting family is that of the arthroscholes, whose segments carry articulated, chitinoidal blue armor. Thus protected, they may grow to lengths of more than a meter.

"Insectoid" soon became shortened in daily language to "secto," and is as loosely applied as ever "insect" and "bug" were on Earth. There are countless kinds of secto. Among the famous are the glitterwing, like a moth whose wings are almost mirrorlike because of tiny metallic particles; a long, many-legged, bulge-eyed scuttler called the I-spy; and the smidgin, which travels in swarms that darken the air, accompanied by flyers that leisurely feast on them.

Marine invertebrates include the drifting gorgon with its mesh of lethal streamers. The big polypus has no definite number of tentacles, for injury causes more than one new one to sprout. When it has grown inconveniently many, the animal develops a second head and set of interior organs, and fissions into two—an alternative to its usual sexual reproduction. Biologists are fascinated by the problem of how this is possible in something of that size and complexity.

Besides male-female sexuality and paired eyes, parallel evolution has produced Cleopatra vertebrates which, like the Terrestrial, have just four true limbs.

Piscoids include the great, sleek, swift, carnivorous pirate and the miter-headed, grotesquely ululating sea preacher. Among marine sauroids is the macrotrach, remarkably similar in appearance to the ancient plesiosaur.

The land is dominated by sauroids. Many of them are more highly developed than any Terrestrial reptile, having efficient hearts, giving live birth and caring for their young, even showing an almost mammalian capacity to learn by experience. This is probably due to the fact that, on generally warmer Cleopatra, being homeothermic ("warm-blooded") confers less relative advantage than on Earth; there do not seem ever to have been any glacial periods. Thus poikilothermic ("cold-blooded") animals have had more chance to flourish and evolve new capabilities.

The best-known ones include: the hipposaur, a hoofed grazer of plains and mountains, as big as a big horse; the king gator, a dry-land carnivore with long legs but otherwise rather crocodilian; the hoplite, a two-meter-wide walking dome of bony armor and spiky tail; the faber, eerily caricaturing humanity in appearance and certain behavior patterns; and the huge-winged flying deltasoar.

The homeothermic beasts remain primitive. They have hair, whose possible colors include a bright green, but no mammary glands. Most young are born with full sets of teeth, immediately able to eat the same as the parents. Where this is not the case, feeding is by regurgitation. Thus even some ground-dwelling animals have beaks rather than snouts, and none have lips.

They are furthest developed in the aerial forms, the ptenoids or pseudobirds. Though none of these quite compare to Terrestrial avians in capabilities, they number some handsome species, like the colorfully plumed jackadandy. The rich-furred (not feathered) flier and diver known as the cinnamon bat is, however, a theroid.

No theroid is very large. A common forest dweller is the tree spook, suggestive of a parrot-billed lemur. On one continent, the carnivorous hootinanny runs in packs which make hideous loud noises in their throat pouches to stampede the prolific herbivorous jumping Toms; both species are rabbit-sized. In arctic regions, the snow snake has shed legs and belly fur in order to go more effectively after its own burrowing prey; with its white pelt everywhere else on the body and its affectionate ways, it makes an excellent pet. Of course, this is only a partial list.

In fact, all these remarks are quite superficial and incomplete. Any planet is a world, and therefore inexhaustible.

THE SERPENT IN EDEN

by Poul Anderson

Regardless, the planet was beautiful.

Even as the aircraft bucked and shuddered, caught in the hurricane shriek, Janne Granstad remembered Cleopatra seen from space. Against night and stars the globe had glowed, blue with its oceans, green, gold, and umber with its lands, swirled silvery with its clouds. The brighter light of the whiter sun made those hues at once more vivid and more serene than Earth's, whose loveliness had always lured tears out upon her lashes. And then the diamond sweep of the ring!

Outside the windows, blackness and lightning raved. Violence toned through metal and bones. The craft lurched insanely, threw her against her seat harness till straps dug into flesh. Arch Fielding turned his head around from the controls. She could just make out his cry: "No use. We haven't got the ceiling to get above this stuff. I'll have to ride it out till—" Janne lost the rest of his words.

She thought, dimly astonished: *That shouldn't be. Should it? No storm should be that tall. But, of course, we aren't on Earth, Earth is nearly 400 light-years south of here. . . . No, wait, "south" doesn't mean the same any longer, Cleopatra doesn't have the same lodestar. . . .*

Roberto de Barros leaned across the narrow aisle between their seats to take her hand. That was almost more bewildering. Or was it? He gave her a stiff smile and said amidst the fury, "Don't be afraid. This is a stout vessel. While we stay aloft, we are safe."

Are we? Janne asked in dread. At once: *No, I must not panic. We have too many unknowns around us to conjure up needless ones. The laws of nature are the same here as they are at home, or in the farthest galaxy. Only the parameters are changed. And not very much. We can live here. We can walk unarmored beneath a sky and breathe an air men have never befouled, we can wash our bodies inside and out with the purity of waters, we can taste the fruits of an untainted soil. Earth today may be more alien to man than is Cleopatra.*

But don't think despair of any kind. Think prose, think science. Her mind almost chanted: *The F7 sun gives us a third again the terrestrial irradiation, a higher proportion of it in energetic particles and quanta. The lower gravity, 0.86, means air pressure dropping more slowly with altitude. The rotation period is less too, seventeen and a third hours, making stronger Coriolis force. The smaller size of the planet may be a factor, bringing climatic zones closer together. And how many more variables have we overlooked? No wonder storms are big, wild, and so unforeseeable by us that this one actually caught us in flight.*

There was courage in the dry recital. But the weather ramped on, and on, and on, driving the aircraft helpless before it.

And when at last clouds broke, sunlight speared through, wind faded as swiftly as it had arisen, Fielding told his companions in a stark voice: "We've gone on too long. Fuel's about finished. I'll have to set us down on the first decent-looking ground I spot."

Peering through the pane beside her, Janne made out crags tumbling toward endless forests. But on the horizon, the sun low above, glimmered what had to be ocean. Then they'd crossed this whole small subtropical continent, caught in the westward half of the cyclone. Base Island lay 2000 kilometers behind. The magnitude of that struck her like a blow.

De Barros said, "Don't be reckless, Fielding. Husband your reserves. Don't descend unless we are all three positive it is safe."

"Shut up," the pilot snapped. "I'll be the judge of that."

De Barros grew rigid. "I think you are exhausted and overwrought," he said. "Granted, you are the most experienced flyer, but not at present the best. Let me take over."

"No!" Fielding yelled, and threw a curse after it.

"Or Dr. Granstad might," de Barros suggested, as if she were not on first-name terms with both men.

Janne shrank back in her seat. "Don't," she whispered. "Please. I—I'm sure Arch can—"

"I was thinking mainly of your welfare," de Barros told her, but had the wit to pursue the argument no further.

Janne took refuge in watching Caesar sink, red and gold, toward the sea without a name. How small the sun was. Or—wait—it was farther away than Sol is from Earth. Otherwise Cleopatra would have been scorched barren. By day one didn't notice the size of the disk—who could look near it?—but when coastal haze gentled its brilliance, the horizon illusion exaggerated the difference—

"Hang on," Fielding said over his shoulder. "Pray if you want. And if we don't make it . . . Janne, I'm glad to have known you."

He gave himself back to his flying. The craft slanted downward. A wide sandy beach appeared in the forward panes, grew with terrifying speed, leaped and struck.

The vehicle bounced. Teeth rattled in jaws. Across hundreds of meters, their dunes and tricky little airs, Fielding brought his machine to a halt.

When peace had thundered upon them, Janne would have flung off her harness and kissed him. But he twisted his neck to confront de Barros and said nastily, "*That's* how come I didn't want you at the console."

De Barros shocked her himself when he replied, cool-voiced, "My compliments on your good luck, at least. Does it extend to establishing communication with Base?"

They knew it did not.

Night was unreined sorcery.

The strand glimmered white, the wilderness behind lifted cupolas of darkness against stars and remote snow-peaks, the ocean before played a million sparkles, light-ripples, glades, and the huge broken ring-image across its ebony. Waves rolled *hush-hush-hush,* the ever gentle surf of Cleopatra. Breezes were mild, bearing alike the smells of salt reaches and green growth. Sand was still warm underfoot, fine enough to yield like flesh caressed. Somewhere, something unknown trilled a song.

Stars glistened in the middle heaven as if to crowd out a black which itself felt luminous. Meteors went among them, streak after silent streak. Northward they were lost in leaping banners of aurora, white, blue, violet, ice green, and ghostly rose. Southward soared the ring. The dust, gravel, and stones which had once been a moon had become a wan rainbow that reached a third of the way up the sky, along which trafficked hasty, flashing, and tumbling jewels in their hundreds. At this season, early winter, the shadow of the planet did not quite scoop out the middle of the arch; the ogive it made was almost visibly rising as night moved onward.

And then lifted Charmian, the larger of the two fragments which men had found worthy of a name. Was the name worthy of her? However tiny, at her nearness she showed as big as Luna seen from Earth. She was less bright—hardly even a globe, rough, scarred, changeable as she spun, though often a scoured spot of metal caught a sunbeam and flared—but she did not have to shine through city fumes and glare; she kindled the waters.

At their edge, Janne roused from her watching to think, guiltily, that she ought not to have wandered from the men. She could see them, distance-dwindled, as they began setting up camp. The glow-stove became an abrupt crimson star. She noticed she was hungry. *Why didn't they call me to come do my share? I drifted away because it seemed they'd be fiddling with the radio and squabbling with each other for hours yet.* In pain: *Why must they, here in a miracle?*

She started back, a tall and limber young woman, yellow hair chopped off below the ears and coverall carelessly worn, but her body possessing the handsomeness of good structure well tended. Being at the core a practical person, as is the duty of any explorer, she answered herself: *Well, it's not a miracle without its troubles and dangers. They're under strain, Arch and Roberto. We could die. That doesn't seem likely, in this moment's majesty; but what will we find tomorrow, or what will find us?*

She knew there was no foretelling. A planet is a world, infinite in the number of its faces and mysteries. The fifty people who *Hanno* had brought were the first who ever saw Cleopatra. Before them, nothing except a robot vessel had made that enormous journey and returned to report its discoveries. They amounted to little more than the fact of an orb which seemed to be habitable and uninhabited. Machines can only find what ignorant men have programmed them to find.

And in the weeks since arrival, the expedition had barely begun to learn. The data which observers aboard the orbiting ship could gather were valuable but lean. Those who went down and established themselves on Base Island had studied it, and the mainland shore opposite, with fanatic intensity; but they had necessarily concentrated on things like the chemistry of rocks and life, rather than topography or natural history. This flight was among the first intended to go farther inland. It was supposed to fare some few hundred kilometers, descending here and there for a closer look, returning within three or four days. Instead . . .

Janne shrugged. Wryness twitched her mouth upward. *We named you better than we knew, Cleopatra. Lovely but—hm—capricious.*

Fielding, who had been hunkered over food preparation, rose as she approached. Though everyone was now too used to the lesser weight to notice it, he, who had been a trifle awkward at home, was graceful here. He was a lanky man with a bush of black hair and features she thought were good-looking in their broad-nosed deep-brown fashion. They had found much in common on the long voyage hither, after they saw it was best to set political differences aside. He remembered with pleasure a visit to her Norway; it was less ruined than most of Earth, he said. She had studied in his North America. Their professions did not really sunder them either, he an engineer, she a naturalist; nobody on this trip could afford to be narrowly specialized.

"Hi," he said. "Want to take over cooking? Short rations need a woman's touch."

"Short?" she asked.

Fielding jerked his head at de Barros, who was raising the tent. "He insists. Says we may be stranded for quite a spell."

The Brazilian left his own work to come and say, "It is an obvious possibility." As always, his slender form was neatly outfitted and soldierly erect. Upon the thin-sculptured head, prematurely gray hair and mustache had gone argent in this light. His English was less fluent that the others', but he spoke it when with them, rather than the official Portuguese or Japanese of the expedition. Janne didn't know whether that was a gesture of friendship or of condescension. Perhaps it was one toward her, another toward Fielding. In spite of the North American's radicalism, she felt she understood him; both their countries remembered not only having once been prosperous and democratic, but having once been satellites of nobody else. Aristocrats, however, were outside her experience, whether baronial Brazilians or magnates of the New Empire.

"You mean," she asked, half timidly, "the radio interference will keep on for long?"

"I am not positive," de Barros admitted. "Our knowledge of stars like Caesar is less than complete. Still, storms upon them have been seen to remain at peak for as much as two terrestrial weeks. Until the present one diminishes, no transmission of ours will carry all the way we have come from Base."

His redundant last sentence made Fielding scowl at what could be a subtle insult. But as if to emphasize, the auroras suddenly flamed high and lurid. The shadows they cast danced across the beach. Janne gasped in awe.

"We are too small to be located from space, and only two of the aircraft have ample range to get here and back, *if* our whereabouts are known beforehand," de Barros continued, likewise unnecessarily. "Hence we must wait till we can send a message and, I suppose, have fuel brought us. It seems common sense to stretch out our food supplies."

Fielding's hand chopped at the forest. "When we've got a whole continent and ocean full of eatables?" he scoffed.

"Are you sure it is?" Janne cautioned.

"Why shouldn't it be? Life uses the same basic stuff everywhere else on a planet. And conditions on this coast don't seem especially different from the east."

"You're assuming a great deal, Arch."

For an instant Janne feared that Fielding would gibe at de Barros with something unspeakably obvious of his own. Perhaps: "Yes, I understand that while similar environments have produced basically similar biochemistries on two planets, the parallelisms couldn't be exact. Cleopatran flesh and fruit lack some of the compounds we must have, like certain vitamins; and a proportion is turning out to be poisonous to us. This has its advantages. It works both ways. Cleopatran diseases can't get a foothold in us. And we *can* supplement our diets, deliciously, if we're careful."

But instead the North American gave her one of his full-lipped smiles and said, "Right. I know what close relatives the potato, the tomato, and the deadly nightshade are. Don't worry. I won't eat anything you haven't certified as a type we checked out on Base and proved was safe. I am betting we'll find a lot hereabouts.

Though such identifications were part of Janne's job, she felt unhappy at the responsibility. Seeking words to explain, she turned her gaze outward, along the shining beach. What she saw made her go taut.

De Barros noticed. *"O que há?"* he exclaimed.

"Shhhh." She pointed.

A hundred meters away, a creature had stepped from the forest onto the sand. Light shimmered off a tall, thin, eerily manlike body. It halted, crouched bent-legged, and peered at the strangers.

She heard a slither as Fielding drew his gun. "Don't shoot," she whispered frantically.

"I'm playing it cautious, no more," he assured her. "Damn, isn't that something!"

All personnel went armed. Thus far there had been no need for it, except to collect specimens. Janne had been glad of that; and, necessary and fascinating though dissections were, she hated seeing slain animals brought to her laboratory shack. It reminded her too sharply of whale and elephant, stag and lion, every kind of wildlife much bigger than a rat or a roach, which Earth knew only in archives. Yonder one, erect, alert, brought back to her some chimpanzees she had once seen in a film . . . O God, almost human faces, faunlike awareness behind the eyes. . . .

Frozen, the forest dweller watched them.

De Barros was first to move, charily, back to a pile of gear. Janne glimpsed him draw forth a pair of night glasses and bring them to focus.

She had never before seen him shaken.

"Madre santa!" burst from him. He dropped the binoculars. She snatched them up for herself. The animal sprang into clear view.

Startled by the noise and movement, it was loping back to cover. In its left hand—not paw, hand—it gripped a rock shaped and edged by what must be chipping.

It vanished. Charmian, entering the shadow of the planet, turned dull coppery-red.

At dawn Janne again strayed off by herself and stood looking over the sea. It had awakened to a million blues and greens, white-laced where waves met land. Out upon some reefs basked scores of great long-necked marine reptiloids. Their numbers bespoke how rich in life these waters must be. The sky, cloudless, was already too lightful for the ring to show, except for a swift phantomlike Iras, Charmian's half-sized companion. But it was not empty, that sky. Thousands of wings shared it with the sun. Clamor drifted down to meet the low surf noise.

Shadows were long, more blue and sharp than on Earth. The air was brisk, barely on the cool side of balmy, laden with fragrances which mostly were different from those of sunset or night.

"Good morning," said de Barros,

Janne turned to greet him. Immaculate, he offered his usual slight bow. "Did you sleep well, since you have risen this early?" he inquired.

"No, I was too excited," she said. "But I don't mind." Impulsively: "I can't get over the—the abundance here. The whole horizon seems bigger." It wasn't in fact, she knew. The equatorial diameter of Cleopatra was 9920 kilometers, 78 percent of Earth's, which meant that, under present conditions, she could see about one kilometer less far.

He surprised her by saying, "It is." After a moment: "This marvelously clear atmosphere. Vision isn't caged by pollution. Perhaps I could show you something comparable on our estate in Rio Grande do Sul, the grasslands. . . . But no." He shook his head. "They are an enclave which will last no longer than our family's wealth and power. Meanwhile, every wind brings filth." He sighed. "Here on Cleopatra—Janne, I begin to understand why my ancestors worshipped the Virgin."

What? she thought. *Is the aristocrat baring his soul?* And then: *No. I shouldn't be sarcastic when he's trying to be friendly.*

It wasn't the first time, either, she recalled. De Barros had found occasion after occasion to talk to her. That wasn't easy. Besides his being a planetologist, a scholar of rocks, magmas, inanimate forces, there was the lack of privacy on Base Island. No two people were ever far from others; it might not be safe. *And, well, Arch has been particularly likely to interrupt.*

"You've seen several new planets," she said, for lack of better words.

"None like this," de Barros answered. "They had their wonders, but men could never make a home on them. A world where we can live, truly live, is more rare and precious than we can well imagine. It is like being given Eden back, to try again."

"Do you think people might colonize here?" It had often been speculated about, but the general feeling was that Caesar was too remote from Sol, at the end of too long a haul. It would never be possible to ship very many emigrants, and they would be more isolated than ever were Pilgrim Fathers—or Greenland Norse, who died out.

"Oh yes, indeed. Let them see our account, and those who can will sell whatever they possess to buy a one-way passage and barely enough equipment for a start."

"But . . . cut off . . . and the uncertainties, the dangers . . ."

"Janne, I can name you a good many persons who would not mind in the least being cut off from our present excuse for a civilization. I rather suspect I am among them. As for danger, in a very few more generations Cleopatra at her worst will be safer than Earth at her best."

"You can't think that: you!" she blurted.

De Barros shrugged. "I am a scientist, who abhors politics and the military. But coming from the family I do, I cannot avoid noticing things, including things the public is not to be told. We are far closer to a far more serious ecological crisis, and the international balance of power is far more precarious, than the insiders admit even to themselves."

Janne winced. "How I hope you are wrong."

He cocked his head. "Forgive me. I didn't mean to distress you on such a gorgeous morning. Let us therefore simply speak of adventure, opportunity, freedom, healthful and beautiful surroundings. Consider yourself. You stand so raptly watching those animals. There must be work for a hundred lifetimes of naturalists. Would you not be happier here than anyplace else?"

Janne bit her lip.

"Why are you sad all at once?" he asked low, and took her arm.

"That being," she got out through a thickness in her gullet.

"Ah. The tool-bearer."

"Yes. I did daydream about pioneering, when it didn't seem Cleopatra had intelligent life. But now . . ."

"Marvelous in truth. To be sure, what we saw appeared less developed than man."

Janne shook her head. "I got a pretty good look at the hand ax. It's made as well as specimens from Earth's Paleolithic were . . . by Homo sapiens. Oh, perhaps you can't teach calculus to the maker. But perhaps you can. And even if not, his breed must be on their way, well on their way, to becoming as bright as we are—their own kind of consciousness, which surely can't be the same as ours."

"You wish to learn more about them, do you not?"

" 'Wish' is a feeble word. I was afire until—Roberto, are you certain colonists will be coming?"

"Yes, if we don't discover some terrible obstacle."

"Maybe we can."

He considered her before saying, "You are afraid that man, permanently on Cleopatra, would destroy the aborigines."

"I am. Think what he did to his fellow men who were weaker, or to the dolphins and apes. I could hope he'd have the sense to learn from Earth and use a new planet right. But don't you see, whatever he did, he'd be *using* it. Making it his, changing it, dominating. . . . He might grant natives a few wretched reservations. No more. What then of their own dreams, everything they might have done, might have given to the universe? No," Janne said through tears, "I don't want to be a party to that. How could I ever dare die?"

She fought for calmness. De Barros ventured to lay a hand on her shoulder. "Easy, easy," he murmured. "You are borrowing trouble. Let us first learn the facts —whatever we can—seeing that we must be here for a while anyway. You have never had a more fascinating challenge, have you?"

"No," she confessed, and felt a surprised gratitude that he should be this understanding. *He's really a good person,* she thought.

"Uh-hum!" said Fielding at their backs. "For your information, I've found where the nearest fresh water is. So how about you making breakfast?"

The men matched fingers to decide who should accompany Janne on her first excursion, and who guard camp. Fielding won; at any rate, he seemed to regard it as a victory. De Barros philosophically said he could study a nearby outcrop. Cleopatran petrology had its duplications of the terrestrial, but already at Base he had discovered differences which a geologist would call spectacular.

The other two collected their equipment. While not planning to go far, they carried compasses—the planet had a stronger magnetic field than Earth—and small transceivers—the electrical chaos in the upper atmosphere wouldn't stop short-range radio, if one didn't mind static. In addition, they bore weapons, first-aid kits, Janne's professional tools, and a couple of sandwiches.

Travel was simple—no tangled brush to fight. Cleopatran plants did not seem to have evolved as far as angiosperms, at least on this continent. However elaborated, they were basically primitive, mostly soft-bodied and disinclined to grow in dense masses. The chief exception was an intensely green stuff which resembled moss (and wasn't), making a springy carpet underfoot.

Janne recognized some of the vegetation. In various cases, she had helped devise the names. Several dinobryons were in sight, upheaving their great spongy masses like coral knolls. A dichtophyte had stretched its network between two of them, strands ranging from cable-thick to thread-fine for the entrapment of animal prey. Metallic particles in the leaves of a Venus mirror made them sheen; the bush was surrounded by insectoids whose wings were similar, and Janne guessed it attracted them to polinate. Nestled beneath the outward-bristling spearpoint stalks of a sarissa, a chameleon plant shifted hue as illumination changed. There were many more kinds of rooted life than these, a few suggestive of ferns, lycopods, fungus, or evergreen trees, most were wildly exotic. Besides every possible shade of verdure, the forest had its bursts of vivid red, purple, yellow—not true flowers, but poinsettia-like pseudoblooms.

It was warm and quiet here, a checkerboard of bright openness and sun-speckled shadow, a multitude of odors sweet, pungent, pleasantly rank. Most of the abundant animals were small and not noisy. Insectoids buzzed or hummed. A swarm of smidgins passed, the tiny individuals merged into a cloud; two leathery-winged reptiloids flapped along, leisurely feasting. A jackadandy flaunted plumes of a sort, though it wasn't a bird either, and trilled. The largest beasts seen were half a dozen hipposaur, grazing at a distance. But Janne was utterly charmed when she came upon a reptiloid new to her, likewise a peaceful herbivore. It could afford pacifism, being a two-meter-wide walking dome of bony armor and spiky tail. "We must call that a hoplite!" she said clapping her hands together.

"Huh?" Fielding asked. "It doesn't look as if it could even hop heavy."

Janne laughed. "An infantryman in classical Greece. Roberto was telling me, several days ago . . ."

"Oh. I'm afraid my education's been neglected. Come on; if you want to search for natives, we should keep moving.

His sourness drew a troubled regard from her. "What's the matter, Arch?"

"Ah, hungry, I guess. That stupid rationing . . . No, that isn't really it. I think you can see what it is."

Her cheeks heated. She decided not to reply. They walked on for a number of minutes.

"Okay, damn it. I'll speak out," Fielding said. "It's that Brazilian bastard, and you getting chummy with him."

"I know you'd overthrow his class, his entire country—and you know I don't agree that violent revolution ever improved anything—but, Arch," Janne pleaded, "we're human beings together, a long, long way from home."

"He hasn't left *his* interests behind. You can bet your blood he's figuring how his relatives can get a stranglehold on this planet—squeeze out the Japanese, sure, but make peons out of the settlers—"

"He isn't! We've talked—"

"Yeah, he wants you in his bag also. Janne, you may be a little naïve, but you're not stupid. You know the signs."

I do, sighed within her. *Inescapable, perhaps. We aren't many women along; and I*—her fingers knotted together—*I'm one of the few who are neither solidly attached to a man nor available to a lot of them. . . . The psychologists should have picked the crew more carefully. Did they try and fail? It must be hard to find qualified volunteers among Earth's poverty-trapped masses.*

Fielding stared before him as he tramped and added harshly, "I suppose you've seen them on me too."

"You—you're sweet," she stammered, "but—"

"But not just what you're after? Who is, then? A rich

Brazilian? I'm not sweet at all. I can be as mean as necessary to keep him from getting you."

Janne bridled. "Arch, you're overstepping."

"No. I'm worried sick. You don't understand how rotten his type is. Why, I'd rather see you the mistress of Captain Yoshida than the wife—the toy, the slave—of—"

"*Nok!* Enough! You're making me understand why Roberto loathes fanatics. Stop slandering him before I stop liking you."

He swallowed. They continued, through a land where she could no longer find beauty.

But after more minutes a new sound broke the silence between them. They halted, strained their ears, stared at each other with anger forgotten. Janne's heart leaped. She beckoned Fielding to follow her, well behind; she could move more quietly than he.

A screen of something like tall bracken rose in front of the clattering. Janne crept up to it, parted stalks and fronds, peered through.

What I thought! What I both hoped and feared it would be.

The creature squatted in a glade where a ridge of flinty rock thrust above soil. It was a reptiloid, hairless; small scales were darkly iridescent in the sunlight. Erect on clawed feet, it would overtop her by a few centimeters. The frame, unobscured by clothes or ornaments, was manlike in a sense. Its alienness—lean barrel of a torso, long, curiously jointed legs, short arms and the way they hung from the shoulder, slender tail—did not make it grotesque; this body had its own grace, its own integrity. The neck was likewise long, flexible, supporting a narrow head. The eyes were its best feature, large and golden, protected by arching ridges that, with the membranous crest on top, made the skull resemble an ancient helmet. The face was flat, a single nostril slit in place of a nose, mouth V-shaped in a perpetual grin, jaws of nearly human delicacy.

When they opened, the variety of teeth indicated that here too was an omnivore.

Here too were hands. They were not hominid. Instead of a thumb, four claw-tipped fingers radiated in a half-circle from the palm. But they worked as well. The Cleopatran was making a *coup-de-poing.*

Janne had studied a little prehistory. She recognized the technique. A bone held in one hand struck pieces off a chunk of rock which the other gripped. The labor went fast, in clash and sparks. The resulting outline would be a thin spear, pointed, sharp-rimmed, about twenty centimeters in length. It would be an all-purpose weapon and tool; the user could throw it to knock down small game, or cut, crush, flense, butcher, scrape, slice, carve. When it grew dull, a new edge was easily put on; when it broke or was lost, a replacement was quickly made. Shards heaped on the pseudomoss showed that generations had used this site.

Hand axes, scarcely to be told from the one taking shape, had been found throughout Earth's eastern half by the many thousands—man's main reliance through tens of millennia.

Man: the tool-bearing animal. Then how can we deny the spirit yonder?

The Cleopatran raised its head and stared. Its tail switched. Fielding joined Janne, his gun held steady. A single explosive bullet could blow the stoneworker in two.

"Don't shoot," she breathed.

"If it acts threatening, I will," he answered. "You're worth more than any glorified snake."

The Cleopatran rose, hefting the almost finished ax and the bone shaper. Despite herself, Janne tensed to duck. However, the being merely regarded them. A breeze brought its musky odor.

She held out her open hands. *"Vi er venner,"* she said. At once the humor of stating "We are friends"—in Norwegian!—kicked a giggle from her, half hysterical.

"He can't know we're not some funny kind of beast," Fielding muttered. "In fact, we are."

"Until we communicate," Janne replied. The thought flitted: *Yes, let's say "he." Cleopatran life has two sexes like ours. I'm not sure which this person is, but "it" isn't right.* She stooped, with an idea of scratching patterns in the ground. The being retreated, vanished in brake and shadows.

"Cautious," Fielding opined. "After all, we're two to one. Maybe he figured you were about to throw a flinder at him. Or maybe he's gone after his buddies. I think we'd better head straight for camp."

Reluctant and disappointed, Janne nonetheless had to agree. She rose and they began walking. "I don't expect they'll be hostile," she argued. "Why should they? The lower animals don't fear us; they've never learned to. . . . Still, I could imagine—well, being trampled by a horde of eager curiosity-seekers."

"Or whatever. I'd feel more trustful if they were mammals."

"Theroids," Janne corrected automatically. "There don't seem to be any true mammals around, just primitive little animals that don't even lactate."

"A cold-blooded, egg-laying thinker. . . . It feels wrong." The engineer grimaced.

"Why? Remember, the reptiloids of Cleopatra—many of them—are further evolved than reptiles on Earth. They have efficient hearts, for instance. I suppose the planet's being warmer, probably never having had an ice age, gives less relative advantage to homeothermic over poikilothermic organisms, so the latter have had more chance to develop onward."

"Homeo—huh?" Fielding scowled. "Never mind. I admit to being prejudiced in favor of mammals. You, no doubt, consider this the most wonderful thing we could have found."

"Of course." Janne hesitated. "Or the most dreadful."

"How that? You don't imagine men have much to fear from a bunch of savages, do you?"

"Yes. They have to fear what they'll be tempted to do." Janne told him her forebodings.

His air of distaste turned to one of reined-in-fury. "And de Barros encouraged you in that sentimentalism? I guess I shouldn't be surprised. It'd make a nice additional excuse—protecting natives—for aristos to keep their feet on settlers."

"What do you mean, Arch?" she exclaimed. "That men should come and . . . take their world away from these people . . . destroy them?"

"If need be. When you've seen, lived with, slum children whose faces were gnawed by rats—and I have —you won't let a bunch of scaly, lipless *things* stand between them and a chance at a decent existence." After a moment: "Oh, I don't advocate extermination, unless we must. We can maintain preserves."

It scarcely eased the horror in her. She had nothing to say while they returned.

Their route was different from before. Near the coast Fielding halted. A stand of dactylophytes, looking like fleshy shrubs, glowed golden-green. "Hey!" he said. Porkplant."

Janne roused from her mood to answer, "Or a close relative."

"Well, for heavens sake, let's collect a bundle and come back after more. Now our bellies won't growl." Analysis and experiment on Base Island had shown that the fronds were tasty as well as nutritious to man —not a complete diet, of course, but a welcome supplement.

"I don't know," Janne said. "We haven't a biochemical laboratory along."

"Why should we need any, for this? Sure, first you put a sample under your microscope and check if it's the exact same species, free of parasites or whatever. I'll bet you a month's pay you'll report positive."

"I wish you wouldn't eat it, Arch."

She failed to dissuade him. In camp, she found he was right about the classification. Nonetheless, she refused a share. De Barros smiled wryly and said, "You may guess whether or not I am disguising cowardice when I declare that if a lady is to go hungry, so will I."

Fielding, his pleasure dashed, glowered at them and grumbled, "Well, at least one of us will keep his strength up." At dinner he feasted ostentatiously.

Next morning a Cleopatran appeared on the beach. It wasn't the same as yesterday's, being of lesser size and having only a rudimentary crest. Janne guessed it was a female, while her previous encounter had been with a male. The creature carried a hand ax of her own. She poised a distance from the aircraft and, when Janne drew slowly near, hissed and made as if to cast the weapon. Janne halted. They exchanged stares for a minute, until the girl tossed a gift of porkplant. The Cleopatran took it up, ate it, and sidled back into the forest.

To de Barros, who had guarded her, Janne remarked, "They really are shy, aren't they? I suppose they think we're supernatural."

"Let us do the traditional thing," the Brazilian suggested: "set forth some trinkets for the next visitor."

Having brought none, they improvised, deciding what could be sacrificed in the way of bright cloth, buttons, a hand mirror, a diffraction grating. It was fun. Janne wondered if they might not be a touch light-headed from hunger, they laughed so much. No, she concluded; it was de Barros' considerable stock of dry humor. The pangs weren't bad, just a continuous reminder that she had a stomach. Tight rationing was not the same as starvation.

It struck them that colored polaroid photographs should make ideal gifts, and they went about looking for good subjects. Fielding found them at that.

In well-fed vigor, he had gone off to try his luck fishing. (The proper word, "ichthyoiding," was unlikely ever to become popular.) His catch had been abundant; one needed merely drop a hook or sweep a net through these swarming waters. When he saw Janne and de Barros side by side, composing a picture of pseudo-blooms, he flung his creel at her feet. "There you are," he snapped.

"What do you mean, Arch?" she asked uncertainly.

His gaze smoldered. "I wanted as many different new species as I could snag for you," he said. Seems like you'd rather hang around camp playing games."

"That isn't fair," de Barros protested. "We are trying to establish communication with the natives."

"Yah, yah, yah." Fielding stalked from them.

Janne spoke in pain: "That isn't like him."

"He does not care for me," said de Barros.

"But he's never been this . . . childish."

"Let him sulk."

The enjoyment was gone from her undertaking. She and the planetologist finished it, though, laying forth their offerings at the spot where the Cleopatran had twice emerged (if it was the same they had spied the night before last). Thereafter they waited. Fielding ate a big lunch, and later sought his sleeping bag for a nap. That wasn't characteristic either.

The return of the being drove concern about him from Janne's mind. The slender, sheening form trod daintily from behind the dactylophytes. Grown less wary of aircraft, tent, and humans, she stopped, peered their way, and neither retreated nor threatened when Janne advanced. "Hasn't she seen our presents?" the girl wondered aloud. She tossed a chunk of porkplant in among them. The Cleopatran promptly went after it, picked it up, and stuffed it in her mouth. When no more was forthcoming, she wandered on down the beach. Bewildered, Janne and de Barros stared after her.

Abruptly she must have noticed signs, for she squatted. Sand flew beneath her scooping hand ax. Soon she reached into the hole she had made and drew forth some equivalent of a clam. With the tool she pried it open and severed meat from the shell. Having eaten, she returned inland.

Man and woman did not speak for a long time.

"I've *got* to learn more," Janne said, over and over, that evening. "Track our visitor down to her community or . . . or whatever we find. It'll be safe, I'm sure. They've been gentle, even timid. But don't you see, this is an impossible paradox, toolmakers who ignore new artifacts. If we don't come to understanding it, who knows what surprises may be sprung on us—back at Base too? Besides, as short of manpower as the whole expedition is, we have a duty to use what time we're bound to spend here."

De Barros opposed her going herself. In the end he yielded, on condition he accompany her. She was much the best suited for such an investigation. He adapted a portable gas detector. Given a fresh scent—the natives left a strong one—and duly adjusted, its meter's needle was as good a tracker as the bloodhounds of history.

Fielding had said little, except to complain that he felt poorly. During the night his illness rocketed.

A sound of vomiting roused Janne. She hastened from her bag and out of the tent. Under the stars, meteors, ring, and aurora, Fielding crouched on the sand. He heaved and shuddered. When she laid arms around him, she felt sweat upon icy skin.

"Roberto!" she wailed. "Wake up, help, help!"

Between them, they got the North American cleansed and brought back into shelter. By the light of their flashbeams, his eyeballs rolled white. Lips pulled parched away from teeth. "Here," de Barros said, "here is a cup of water."

"Not from you," Fielding mumbled. "You poisoned me. Or she did. Lied to me . . . so I wou'n' connerdic' whatever lie she'll tell 'bout this planet to save her damn snakes. . . . Murderers, both o' you—"

Dawn walked russet over the mountains. Waves glittered and whooshed beneath a salt breeze. Winged life went aloft in its thousands.

Outside the tent, where Fielding lay in feverish sleep, Janne and de Barros traded looks. "You didn't believe what he accused me of, did you?" the man rasped.

"Of course not." She shook his hands.

"I am not . . . ruthless. Neither are my kinfolk. He sees us as tyrants and schemers. He cannot see troubled people trying their clumsy human best to cope with a worsening world."

"I can, Roberto. I don't think your way of coping is always right, but your good will I've never doubted—nor that of the Japanese." In a rush: *"I'm* the one who poisoned him! I told him those plants were probably safe."

"If that is the trouble."

"What else could it be? And they seemed so—so identical in every way with—"

De Barros frowned and chewed his mustache. "Precisely. I admit to thinking you were overcautious, and only followed your example because—*Bem,* never mind why. Don't blame yourself. You did your best, short of telling him a falsehood. Besides, it may well be something else. He may have picked up an infection. We have not absolutely proved that no indigenous germ can affect us. Or he may have been exposed to a factor that we were too, but had an idiosyncratic reaction. Without intensive clinical study, there is no telling."

"Then there's no treatment." She swallowed hard.

He nodded. "Nothing but supportive treatment, and prayer that his body can throw off the effects by itself."

"We have a whole damn pharmacy along."

"But what drug to use?" de Barros reminded her. "What antibiotic might work on a Cleopatran microbe? Or if this is an allergy, do we want antihistamine, antivenin, or what? If it is an organ-specific toxin, which does it attack and what is the antidote?" He clenched his fists. "We dare not medicate on a guesswork basis. Most drugs have side effects. We could too easily touch off a synergism, where between them the disease and the 'cure' kill him. And while this radio blackout lasts, we can't even get professional advice."

"How does he seem to be doing—honestly?" Janne made herself ask. As a venturer onto several different worlds, de Barros had acquired a good deal of practical knowledge.

The Brazilian's tone bleakened further. "Not well. Pulse, respiration, temperature, nausea, diarrhea, and the resulting dehydration . . . he is sinking."

"O God, O God." Janne almost cast herself upon his shoulder. But instead—she didn't quite know the reason—she went off to weep alone.

The native came back.

Janne, huddled on a rock, was first aware of it when sand scrunched. Looking up, she saw the neat dinosaurian shape close to her, ax loosely held, mouth smiling wide as if in anticipation.

"Why—why, Cleo," she stammered, and scrambled to her feet.

The other being stood a minute longer. Receiving no food, she turned and departed. Her stride took her right over the gifts which lay, gaudy and forgotten, on the shore of the sea which had no name.

It struck through Janne: *Couldn't I follow, observe? It may not be entirely wise to go alone. Still, anything's better than waiting useless for Arch to die.*

She hastened to fetch the sniffer. De Barros had barely noticed what went on. Hands caught white-knuckled behind his back, he paced in circles around the tent. His face seemed well-nigh as haggard as that of the unconscious man within.

"I'm going after Cleo," Janne said.

De Barros surfaced from his broodings. "No, you

mustn't without a partner, and we can't leave our comrade."

"One can tend him as well as two for a short while. I'll be careful. There isn't any danger, really. I can't get lost in those open woods, with the sun for a guide. If I should be attacked, besides my gun, I have my legs. I can outrun any reptiloid." In a surge of gallows mirth: "Remember, nature designed me to weigh ten kilos more than I do here."

"Nevertheless—" De Barros broke off. It was as if suddenly he no longer saw or heard her.

"I won't be gone long," said Janne hastily into the silence that she took for consent. She hurried off in pursuit of the native. Once she cast a glance behind. The Brazilian stood motionless, staring out over the ocean.

She wondered briefly what had entered him, but dropped that question in the excitement of the chase. Though Cleo had disappeared, where tracks in sand met vegetable mat, the detector needle pointed straight inland. Movement was swift through that parklike forest. Presently she saw the being's head bob and sway above a row of fronds.

Cleo glimpsed her in turn and halted. For a dizzy moment Janne thought, *Maybe at last she'll give me a sign.* The creature wandered on. Frustration tasted harsh in Janne's throat. She followed at a discreet distance.

Why do they all but totally ignore us? Maybe they believe that's how to treat gods or demons. . . . No. They've been careful about us, but not frightened. She took food from me. Why did she spurn our other offerings?

Cleo drifted in no special direction. She dug up and ate a sugarroot. She spied a small theroid on a branch overhead and cast her ax. It missed; the animal scuttled off; she retrieved the weapon and continued her stroll.

Where is the male we met? Where are any more whatsoever? . . . Oh!

Cleo stopped dead. Her tail stiffened. Out from a clump of bushes, jerky, jaunty, shining in sunlight, came a young one of her kind. It could be nothing else, a miniature, half a meter tall, carrying its own doll ax. *The darling!*

Janne screamed.

Cleo had hissed and hurled. The baby saw. Barely in time, it sprang aside, wheeled, and fled. Cleo bounded after. She grabbed her weapon on the run. Stems bent, branches snapped. Jaws agape, she bounded in chase.

Horror roared around Janne.

Comprehension exploded it. She sank to the ground and shrieked forth laughter like a woman gone crazy.

Caesar, blazing its rapid way across heaven, stood to westward. The ocean flashed gold above sapphire, turquoise, and arabesqued alabaster. Sands shone, forest glowed, snowpeaks lifted in purity. Wings rode upon crystalling, flowing air.

In that hugeness, vehicle and camp seemed flecks which a stray wind had blown in and would soon blow away again forever. Janne's heart twisted when she saw how de Barros had erected instruments to observe the sun. *Poor haunted man, he needs his own place to hide,* she thought, and quickstepped toward him.

Yet, spying her, he dropped the screen on which he had been projecting a magnified disc. He ran. His hair tossed gray and wild. He grabbed her to him and kissed her. "Janne, it worked, it worked!" jubilated in her ear. "Already he is conscious, clear in the brain, *sim,* he has a little strength and—you did it, you, you, you!" He let her go, save for taking her hand. "Come. He would like to see you."

In the yellow dimness of the tent, she knelt by Fielding's bedroll and sobbed for joy. He gave her a shaky smile. His voice was still barely audible. "Hi, honey. Want to cook me a bowl o' soup in a while? You pick the recipe."

"You are getting well?" It was a stupid question, but she had just been snatched out of anguish.

"Yeah. Ol' Doc de Barros thinks I'll be on my feet in three-four days. Now that the poison's leaving me, I can take cell stimulants and . . ." His mien turned anxious. "Janne, can you and . . . and Roberto . . . ever forgive me?"

"For what? You were sick, dear Arch." She brushed lips across his. "What you can do for us is take care of yourself."

"I obey. I've learned. From here on in, I listen to you." Fielding uttered a chuckle. "Funny. Eden . . . forbidden fruit . . . this time the man tasted, 'spite o' the woman. . . ." His words trailed off.

De Barros touched her. "Come," said the Brazilian. "Let him rest. It is a natural sleep."

Outside, she drew breath after breath until at last she could say levelly: "Then it was the porkplant."

"Well, yes and no." de Barros replied. "You gave me the clue."

"Me? How in the universe?"

"Granted, a chance remark of yours. However, I have an idea that chance favors those who deserve well. When you were running off—do you remember what you said to me about your weight on Cleopatra?"

"Um-m-m . . . yes, since you mention it . . . but what—" Janne sat down on a dune and hugged her knees. "Tell me."

He joined her. "It triggered something," he explained. "Perhaps I would have gotten the thought anyhow, but probably not in time. Arch was failing fast. I was desperate enough to try anything, if only I could find the least clue.

"Well. Cleopatra is smaller than Earth, therefore its gravity field is weaker. But that weakness is not in proportion. If the two planets had the same density, we would weigh less here than we do. And, actually, if they had the same composition, Cleopatra should be somewhat less dense, because of a smaller mass compressing itself less at the core. In fact, the mean density is ten percent *more* than Earth's. This must be due to a greater proportion of heavy elements, as the spectrum of Caesar also indicates. Doubtless this whole system condensed later than Sol's, from a nebula which had had time to accumulate more large atoms. For Cleopatra, that means more radioactivity, a hotter interior, hence the outgassing of as much atmosphere as we have around us—" De Barros shook himself. "I babble. You know all this. I too am a little silly from happiness."

"Go on," she urged.

"You recalled the fact to me," he said. "I realized that there must be surface regions where heavy elements happen to be especially concentrated. There are on Earth. Plants in such areas may take up the metals and become toxic. For example, locoweed—selenium-contaminated desert forage—is a menace to livestock. I heard about that from a bailiff on our estate. . . . If this can happen on Earth, how much more often on Cleopatra?"

Janne straightened. "By glory, Arch's symptoms did look like arsenic poisoning, didn't they? Now that you've pointed it out!"

"I am not sure what element is responsible," de Barros said. "Perhaps several. A broad-spectrum chelating drug did the—ah, did the trick."

He paused before continuing: "I have found that the solar storm has passed its maximum. I estimate we can get a call through in about six more days—C-days, that is. Therefore we can give Arch adequate nourishment without starving ourselves too much—" he grinned—"or resorting to organically grown foods."

"Splendid," said Janne absently. Her mind had gone elsewhere. "Animals must have an immunity, whether or not a given soil is metal-bearing. The possibility will be a hazard for humans. Not too bad. It simply means people must check a region before they settle in it, and take what precautions are indicated."

Surprised, de Barros said, "What? Have you resigned yourself to colonization?"

Janne laughed. "Goodness! I'm sorry, Roberto. Your news made me forget I haven't told you—or Arch. He'll be so glad. In spite of his . . . his ideas about human supremacy . . . or his dislike of 'glorified snakes' . . . I can't believe he was really single-minded about us overrunning a whole other sentient race."

"Wait a minute." De Barros seized her arm. "Do you mean the Cleopatrans are *not* intelligent?"

She nodded. "I should have deduced it earlier. Besides the youth of this world, its generally primitive biology, there was the toolmakers' absolute lack of interest in communication, lack of curiosity, lack of community. My guess is, they're solitary. Individuals stake out territories, sharing the flint sources. Male and female meet just in mating season. Yes, I should have realized they aren't thinkers, long before I did. What clinched it was seeing a small one fending for itself. Consciousness demands learning, which demands parental care. The lowest mammals and birds look after their young. Cleo . . . The moment she saw this hatchling, she wanted to eat it."

De Barros sat appalled.

"It escaped," Janne said. "Don't be shocked. I was at first, till I realized what the significance was. They're as unconscious, you might say innocent, as fish or praying mantises."

"But they make tools!" he protested.

"That was what blinded me too," she replied. "We know we evolved with tools in our hands. Naturally we supposed that whatever other kind of life uses them must be like us, or at least like our near ancestors."

She sighed. "The truth is," she continued slowly, as

if to herself, "we're unique, on our planet, only because we've destroyed our brothers. In that moment I remembered what I'd read or seen filmed from long ago when they lived: a sea otter pounding an abalone open against a stone he held on his chest: a beaver colony damming a river; a chimpanzee shaping and wetting a straw to catch termites with. . . . At that, we still have termites, and the other ants, and the bees. They still do things which are much more complicated than chipping stones into one particular shape.

"Not that these—what shall we call them? Fabers? Not that they aren't wonderful, and important, and with many truths to teach us. How I hope the people who come will spare them."

She rose, walked from him, gazed out across the sea to its clear and burning horizon. "Eden," she finished. "We are the serpent."

2300 A.D.

A world grew in all directions from the place of landing. People became different from one another, moving away to create different places and life-styles, filling up the world. Cleopatra changed. Local flora and fauna retreated before the life from Earth. Two great powers gradually emerged to rule the planet, Dardania in the north of the western hemisphere, Pindaria in the east. Together these two nations controlled most of Cleopatra's land masses; and what they did not control, island chains and remote mountain settlements, they sought to influence, with a view toward future annexation.

Fabers were first modified in Dardania. In the beginning they became workers and servants; later they served as dancers and musicians, taking part in the developing Dardanian art forms. At the same time both Dardania and Pindaria continued with covert biological research on the faber form, seeking modifications that might have war applications. Much of this work was senseless, carried out to satisfy the individual bent of the researcher, who in many cases held a dubious scientific competence.

The story of Marcus Binh perhaps sums up the human reaction to the conflict of art, society, and misguided science . . .

—Hela Fenn, Psycho-Soc
Colonial Survey, 3300 A.D.

FABER-MASTER

by Michael Orgill

Leaping across the stage, the thesp executed an *entre-chat-douze*. Then he bouréed to the center of the stage and stood motionless on point as a holo-camera dollied in for a close-up. The thesp's golden eyes sparkled in the glare of the arc lights.

"Enough," Marcus Binh said, and the crew stopped taping.

I can use it, he thought. The thesp was an Unger, the most primitive of faber breeds. Binh had thought that the reptile did not have the ability to follow an *entrechat* with a *bourée,* but the dance had gone better than he had hoped. It had taken longer than most; the thesp had required three days of coaching. What else could he expect of a second-rate animal?

He saw Osbeck standing next to a camera. Binh averted his eyes. Best not to give the assistant coach too much credit before the production ended. The man simply could not handle it. Osbeck had coached the thesp. He had been right about the animal's capabilities. Now he would expect Binh to give all his other ideas a respectful hearing.

Osbeck was not one to slink away with his own private satisfactions. Binh sat on a rickety canvas-backed chair, surrounded by a crowd of technicians. Osbeck threaded his way toward him.

"We can use this thesp again," Osbeck said.

Binh said nothing. He looked at the stage where the thesp lay on a stretcher. Two medics taped wires to his skull which led to a bank of monitoring equipment.

Dymund, the chief technician, whispered in Binh's ear as Osbeck waited for an answer. There was a power interruption. It would take at least fifteen minutes to trace the source of the breakdown. Already cumulus clouds were turning purple and massing everywhere in the sky. The slightest rainfall would make taping impossible.

Binh stood up abruptly. "Does the thesp have a name?" he asked Osbeck.

Osbeck wiped his forehead with the back of his hand. "It's in the papers somewhere. I'm sure of it. But it doesn't matter. He's the most perfect Unger I've ever seen. You can see that."

A technician pressed a clipboard in Binh's hands. He signed it after a cursory glance. He began to make his way through the milling technicians, and Osbeck followed at his side.

"He is an Unger," Binh said after a moment, "but not perfect." The clouds were a threat. It might be less than fifteen minutes before it rained.

"But you have to admit that the thesp was beautiful," Osbeck said. "Believe me, I really made a buy. Took two days on the market to close the deal. We can use the thesp for any number of scenes. I see him in a comedic improvisation . . ."

"I won't use the thesp again," Binh said. "Your coaching was fine, Osbeck, better than I expected, but trade the thesp in. There's no other place for the animal."

Osbeck wandered slowly away as Binh began conferring with a group of lighting technicians. The man was intolerable, Binh thought. Osbeck had been a thesp coach for five years. He could handle brief scenes well, but he was a failure at choreographing longer dances. Binh was surounded by Osbecks. Every coach on the production was trying to gain Binh's confidence, as if he would yield some of his control to a favorite and agree to fashion a collaboration.

Binh entered his office tent. He filled a stone basin with water and splashed it on his face. After drying with a rough towel, he lowered himself on his brown meditation cushions and assumed a half-lotus.

It was getting more and more difficult to concentrate. The first signs had appeared months ago when he began the production. He had thought it would go like all the others. This one, however, had not been a product of his vision alone. Cleopatra would have its bicentennial in less than six months. This production had been commissioned by the planetary council to be the centerpiece of the celebration.

Thoughts chattered. The council had difficulty uniting the contending factions behind this innocuous project. Every group on Cleopatra was represented in the crew, in line with quotas ordered by the Council. Hispanics from the southern hemisphere. Japanese from the volcanic archipelagos. Europeans and Asiatics from the heartland of Dardania. Chinese, Vietnamese, and other Orientals from Pindaria. Blacks from the island continent of New Africa.

Binh had worried about the possibility of rivalries, but there had been no problems. On any project there would be professional jealousies, and the ethnic mix could have made them more intense. Everything, however, had gone smoothly. The Council propagandists held up the production as an example of global cooperation, but Binh thought differently. The crew, happy to land this plum of a job, laid aside their political and ethnic differences. The work had come first.

The air in the tent was oppressively humid. Binh inhaled deeply. Vague pains shot through his chest. The cushion leather creaked as he shifted his weight. Closing his eyes, he began to meditate.

Count one, two, three, four. It was a technique Binh had used since his student days. He concentrated on the numbers, assigning one to each inhalation. When thoughts appeared he let them float away. Count one, two . . . there was a babble of voices outside the tent . . . three, four . . . only a few minutes more . . .

A sudden light stung his eyes.

"Weather looks bad." The production's meteorologist stood in the opening.

Binh ran his hand over his skull. "How much time?"

The meteorologist shrugged. "I don't give us more

than a half hour of clear weather. You might get more. It depends."

It was twilight. A blaze of arc lights illuminated the location. Stepping out of the tent, Binh was immediately surrounded by journalists. Their shouted questions rose to a din. He tried to push his way through, but the journalists pressed closer. He could not move as the vid cameras and microphones were waved in his face.

Osbeck was among them, waving a sheaf of papers. He tried to force them into Binh's hands.

"Please reconsider," he said. "I have everything here, the thesp's genetic pedigree, a full report of the lab tests. You'll see he's a first-rate animal."

Osbeck's obsequious voice irritated him. Binh pushed the papers away. He managed to break free, and shoved through the crowd. The throng followed like insects.

"Maestro," a reporter shouted over the babble, "do you expect the Council to withdraw support now that Kevin Hussein is chairman?" The journalist wore a white helmet with a tiny video cube attached to the top. Jostled by the crowd, he kept his head turned toward Binh, so that he would always be within the cube's range.

Binh said nothing. Other voices drowned out the first questioner. "Do you admit you've exceeded budget?" a frizzy-haired woman asked. Binh remained silent, infuriating the reporters. They encircled him again. Everyone began shouting at once. Binh raised his hands, but the pushing and shouting grew louder. Hands holding cameras and microphones reached out and jabbed his body.

"Do you expect Hussein to ask for script changes?" someone asked. A thin, male reporter held a microphone under Binh's nose. "Have you been ordered to use human dancers?" he shouted. "That would be impossible," Binh said, brushing the microphone away.

"Would you resign if the Council issued that order?" another journalist asked.

"Let me pass," Binh shouted. "This is not a press conference." Shoving through the crowd, members of his crew moved toward him. Fistfights broke out among journalists vying for better positions. Still cameras were thrust above the crowd by reporters unable to push their way forward. A burly, red-haired man in a purple jump suit blocked Binh's way. Waving his arms, he shouted an unintelligible question.

Simon, one of Binh's electricians, shoved the man away. Three of Simon's assistants joined him and linked arms around Binh. The journalists continued to shout questions as the men escorted Binh out of the crowd.

"Binh's finished. Hussein will see to that!" a tall man shouted. He wore a blue tunic, the uniform of Hussein's political party. The din grew louder. The reporters began to shout the heckler down.

"Are you going to meet with Hussein?" a journalist called out.

"Binh doesn't have the guts!" another heckler shouted.

The crew members hurried Binh along, and the crowd ran behind them. Binh wanted to shout an answer which would stun them all into silence. But it would get back to Hussein. Binh did not want to give Hussein anything to use against him.

Simon grabbed Binh's elbow and kept him moving. Despite his escort, the crowd still pressed against him. Binh gasped for air. A woman leaned against him, her breasts brushing his left shoulder. Binh stared at her face. He studied the network of wrinkles under her eyes.

She grimaced and began to pummel him with her fists. The crowd drove itself toward the stage, sweeping Simon and the other crew members away from him. Cameras and recording equipment dropped to the ground and smashed to pieces. A woman spit in Binh's face. A blue triangle, the emblem of Hussein's political organization, was sewn on the top of her jumpsuit. Why were so many of his supporters here? Binh thought.

As the crowd pushed and shoved around him, Binh managed to remain standing. Random blows struck him, and he covered his head with his arms. Something hit him on the back of his neck. His vision went black for a moment, and his head began to pound.

Binh was pushed down violently. His knees scraped against the ground. Boots slammed into his body. He rolled himself into a fetal ball. The blows glanced off the curve of his back.

He had taught himself this defensive position in his student days. He had been emeshed in the "Months of Revolution" which preceded the collapse of the First Council. Every day had been filled with significant events; Binh, along with the other members of the Common Front, had thought he had the power to make history. Cleopatra had become theirs; it would never be the same again.

Every thought and action had contributed to the struggle. Binh, who had been an apolitical aesthete, made himself into a street fighter. In spite of his myopia and slender body, he had become a karate expert, using to good effect the grace and stamina he had acquired in his studies of dance. He had transformed his body into a precision instrument, and with it he had served the struggle.

A gust of wind whistled through the crowd. Binh could withstand their blows indefinitely—soon they would forget him in their confusion. He felt drops of rain splattering on his back, and the distant booming of thunder. A downpour soaked through his jumpsuit. The crowd scattered, running for the shelter of the public buildings.

As Binh stood up, pain shot through the small of his back. He felt the moistness of a bruise, and the pain increased. Simon ran up to him, grabbing his elbow as if he were about to collapse. Brushing him away, Binh walked back to his tent unsteadily, letting the droplets of rain run down his face. The technicians were erecting a protective dome over the stage as the storm gathered force to sweep in from the eastern seaside.

Binh gazed out of his tent's plastic window. The storm lashed the boulder-strewn beaches with icy surf. The clear weather had been an interval between storms. The rain beat against his tent more violently. He called Juan Bianco, his production assistant, on the intercom.

"Yes." Bianco's abrupt voice crackled over the line.

"Juan, this is Binh. I want to spend the night in First City. When is the next helicopter leaving?"

"It isn't. The storm has grounded everything. The bay is too choppy for hoverboats."

"Then get a room for me. I'll drive right over."

"All right, but there's a problem." There was a tinge of irritation in his voice. "Some coaches are taping on their own." Binh heard a babble of voices in the background.

"I'm coming over," Binh said, cutting off the intercom. For a moment, he stared through the window in confusion. No one had the authorization to tape without his permission. All the coaches knew that. What could they be thinking of?

He rushed through the rain to his land car, and drove it toward the public buildings. The lowering clouds were purple verging on black. Lightning pulsed through them.

The rapid change of weather made him feel as if he were losing control. When the Council had given him this assignment, he had been afraid it was too big for him to handle. Binh had made his reputation on small productions. He had never supervised more than three coaches, and his budgets had been minuscule compared to the one he was now juggling.

Embrace the Swords, the holo which had made him

famous at twenty-three, was produced with only one assistant. He had used a crew of three on *The Untold Want,* which most critics considered his masterpiece. On that production, he had lighted the stage himself, and had operated a camera on almost every take.

On this production Binh directed a huge crew. He sometimes felt powerless, as if the production's momentum would snatch control of the project out of his hands.

Bianco met him with an umbrella at the entrance to the public hall. He was swarthy, with thick lips and a broad nose. He stroked his bald head as he always did when a situation had passed beyond his control.

"I'm glad you got here so quickly," Bianco said. A confusion of voices floated down the hall from the interior of the building. Bianco glanced nervously over his shoulder, turning back to look at Binh with an exasperated expression.

Entering the building, they walked down the corridor toward the public hall, where some sets had been erected. Binh had heard a crew member call Bianco "Binh Junior," and he now realized that the description fit. Bianco wore a white jumpsuit like his own. Binh suspected that his assistant's baldness was not natural. The man probably shaved his head to match Binh's own hairlessness.

Halfway down the corridor, Bianco touched his elbow, moving to block his way.

"I think you should go in there knowing what's happening," Bianco said. "When I realized the storm would lock us in for the rest of the night, I set up some more equipment. We could use it to tape scenes if the weather hadn't cleared up by tomorrow. That way, we could have some sequences down, and it would take less work once we got outside. We got all the equipment in place and Sobrino went berserk."

"Sobrino?"

"Hussein's representative. She has credentials from

the Council, but since Hussein is financing our cost overrun, she answers directly to him."

For a moment, Binh's mind was a blank. The name meant nothing to him. Then a memory flashed through his mind.

Dia Sobrino. Benito M'Wabe, the critic, had introduced her at the party he had given in Binh's honor at the beginning of the production. Amusement had flashed in the critic's eyes as Binh and the woman had shaken hands. M'Wabe had continued to speak in his simpering voice, but his words merged into the general babble as Binh stared at Sobrino's face. The woman stood with her arms akimbo, her face framed by a mass of frizzy brown hair. Binh had rarely been in contact with a woman who projected such overwhelming sexual energy. She looked at him with piercing black eyes. He kept glancing away in embarrassment, his eyes roaming over her muscular, khaki-clad body. Her large breasts were covered by a leather halter, and a silver-studded belt encircled her narrow waist. The woman's beauty intimidated him, as if at bottom he could never be at peace with it.

"She and Benito M'Wabe heliocoptered in from First City during the clear weather," Bianco was saying, "while we were taping."

Binh could hear shouts coming from the public hall. He tried to move down the corridor toward them, but Bianco once again blocked his way.

"I think you should know more," he said.

"Well, what are they doing?"

"Sobrino is fronting for Hussein. Officially, the Council is funding the production, but now the truth is out. Half the original funding was his. Now he's picking up the overrun. That gives him total control. He intends to keep a close watch."

A cheer echoed down the corridor. It sounded as if an audience had gathered in the public hall to watch some spur-of-the-moment entertainment.

"Hussein," Binh said absently. "That mob of reporters kept asking me about him. I've assumed Hussein was behind the Council all along. That's nothing new."

"That's not all,' Bianco said abruptly, as if impatient with Binh's lack of comprehension. "Sobrino is dangerous. I've seen her type in operation. She's the purest of fanatics. She'd do anything for Hussein. He is financing Scientific Transcendence, he's their charismatic leader. They advocate bringing to humans the kind of bio-engineering we use on fabers. We fought those battles twenty-five years ago. We won, but the other side's back, and they're strong. We're lucky most of the production is in the can. Hussein's close interest in us can only mean that he's about to make demands. He might intend to use us as a propaganda ploy to force the Council to decontrol faber engineering and allow its application to humans. It's the only reason I can see for his support of the production."

Suddenly Osbeck appeared in the hall, staggering toward them as if he were drug-intoxicated. "Binh!" he shouted. "Tell your damn son to keep his hands off my work!" He paused, propping himself against the wall.

"That's the other thing," Bianco said. "Your son is here. He arrived sometime after Sobrino and M'Wabe. I don't know how. He's joined Hussein's faction, and Sobrino's taken him over. They're both in there turning everything upside down."

"Damn right," Osbeck said, his voice slurring. "That son of a bitch took my faber right off the stage in the middle of a drill. He said I didn't have the right . . ."

"Shut up, Osbeck!" Binh said. He felt like hitting the coach, but it would serve no purpose.

"Maestro," Bianco said, "we've got to get in there. We've got to stop whatever they're doing."

Binh turned, nodding. Bianco followed as he hurried down the hall toward the sound of cheering.

A group of technicians blocked the entrance. Binh

did not recognize any of them. They had probably been among the group of sound mixers who had arrived from First City two or three days before. Lounging in the doorway, they wore white smocks. The sign of their guild was tattooed on the back of their left hands, a jagged, blue bolt of lightning.

Binh and Bianco came to a halt and stood before them. There was amusement in the technicians' eyes as they looked at him. For a moment, nothing was said. He had an urge to shout at them; the disrespect in their faces was plain. He wanted them to shrink away from the door with fear in their eyes. Then he could make a proper entrance into the hall.

There was no need to shout. Bianco gestured, and the technicians moved aside to clear a path for them. As Binh walked past them, his body tensed. The technicians loomed over him. He felt the warmth of their breaths as if the exhalations might burn his skin. Another wave of cheering and applause came out of the hall. Osbeck shouted something behind him, but the uproar drowned out his words.

The hall was a jumble of people and equipment. The control room was located on a balcony which ran around the upper hall. Binh could see technicians working behind the soundproof glass as if taping were underway. Their faces were illuminated by the lights of their instruments.

A crowd of idle crew, journalists, and hangers-on were massed in a circle, applauding and cheering. Binh could not see what was driving them into such a high pitch of enthusiasm. They were talking excitedly among themselves; no one noticed him.

A hand squeezed his left shoulder. "I was wondering what took you so long to arrive," a voice said.

It was Benito M'Wabe. The critic smiled slightly, revealing a row of broken teeth. He wiped a gleam of perspiration off his upper lip with an ornate, white and gold silk handerchief.

"What's happening here, Benito?" Binh was glad to see M'Wabe in the midst of this confusion. The critic had given him his first favorable reviews, and had taken his side when *The Untold Want* aroused its initial storm of controversy. Since the early days, M'Wabe had always supported him in print, praising his talent even during the fallow period after the disaster of *Robes of Repentance,* when most of the other critics had deserted him.

"You are truly remarkable, maestro," M'Wabe lisped. "I had no idea you had opened yourself to such innovation. I have only seen such things in back alleys, among the desperate young. I haven't dared to write about these performances—even a champion of the avant garde has to have some assurance he is right—but here you are, boldly leading the way. And on a government project."

"Benito, what are you talking about?"

"Maestro, you needn't be coy. I will not leak any word of this stunning breakthrough until I have your authorization."

The crowd broke into applause again, and M'Wabe beamed paternalistically. His wide nostrils flared as he smiled at Binh. Wrinkles furrowed his forehead.

"But you will," M'Wabe said after a moment, "give me an exclusive interview, before any critical jackals pollute your intentions with their stupidity and ignorance?"

Binh glanced up at the control room. A technician clapped his hands together once, the signal that a taping had been completed. He then moved his right finger in a circle, signaling that the holo just taped was about to be replayed.

Binh felt angry, but tried to let the feeling pass. M'Wabe gestured at him again, but Binh walked away before the critic could speak. The crowd was disbanding, and he wanted an open view of the replay area.

He looked for Philip in the crowd. Why had Philip

not come to him as soon as he arrived on the island? He had last seen his son two years ago. The meeting had been brief. Philip, without consulting him, had dropped out of the Thespian Institute. He had intended to go into the Pindarian Mountains where he would live on a spiritual commune.

A chill went through Binh as he remembered. There had been nothing to say. Philip had told him of his plans, with a look of defiance, as if he had expected Binh to oppose him. But Binh had been involved in a project. There had always been a project. Had it been *Remembered Sins?* Binh was horrified that he could not recall. He had not argued with Philip, as if his son had been a stranger.

Standing before the replay area, Binh let the memories fade. The floor sensors flickered as the machine was readied for projection. If M'Wabe was so enthusiastic, he thought, why should I be apprehensive? The crowd gathered around him, buzzing with excitement. They had already seen whatever was to be projected here. Nothing was real for most of them unless they could see it holoed.

M'Wabe came over to stand beside him, clasping his hands together as if he were a chef presiding over a steaming banquet table.

"Speaking frankly, maestro," he said, "you are a selfish man. After all, keeping your son's talent from me, your greatest admirer, for all this time."

The hall filled with "ahs". Two columns of mist rose up in the replay area as the room went dark. A rainbow of sparkling dots rapidly suffused both columns as the holotape leaders ran through the playback machines. Binh felt the anticipation of the crowd, and wondered why two tapes were being played simultaneously.

Glancing over to the spot the crowd had abandoned, he saw holo-cameras grouped around only one performance area. He was angry once again. Surely some comparison was to be made—one of the unedited performances he had taped was being run. He would fire the person responsible for this. Only he could authorize the playing of a tape or the taping of a performance.

The sparkling dots gradually faded, and the indentifying codes flashed up and down the columns. The left holo was the first to clear. Binh's image appeared in the center of the column. He made a beckoning gesture, and made notes on a clipboard.

Bianco appeared at his side, taking Binh's attention away from his representation in the holo projection.

"I couldn't do anything to stop this," Bianco whispered in his ear. "They have written authorization from the Council."

Binh waved for him to be silent, turning back to the projection. The right column was still shimmering with multicolored dots, but he knew the left holo well.

It was the "Inner Tape," the centerpiece of his production. In it, two thesps, a male and female, danced an allegory of Cleopatra's colonization. All the other mimes and dances reflected and expanded on it.

The technicians were projecting a middle section of the "Inner Tape." Since a final version had not been edited, Binh was visible at the beginning of the shot, as he prepared to give the unseen thesps their starting signal.

A splice in the tape ran through the machine. Binh's image jumped, and disappeared. An image of a male and female thesp abruptly replaced it.

Bianco whispered to him again. "I didn't know they'd gotten hold of this tape. I don't think the control room crew is responsible. Sobrino must have forced it on them with her damned Council authorization."

The right column began to clear. A cloud of glimmering particles coalesced into a three-meter-tall image of Philip. He had his arm around a short, muscular woman. It was Dia Sobrino. They both wore black leotards. The fabric strained against the curves of her breasts. Philip stared blankly into the camera as Sobrino lightly stroked his brown, curly hair.

On the left tape, the thesps began their dance. Jason was a Resnick, the most humanoid of the breeds. He stood silently as the superimposed face of Jasmine, his partner, swam up to fill the entire holo column. She represented Cleopatra as it was before the human colonization, when none of her species dominated her. Jasmine was one of the finest Ungers with which he had ever worked. He had coached her personally, emphasizing facial mimes which would suggest the aboriginal faber. The Unger breed was perfectly fitted to this task, since its genetic pool contained so many primitive features. Most of his contemporaries would not use Ungers because their tails had not been completely bred away; their appearance in a production smacked of the retrograde, the sentimental. For Binh's Inner Tape, however, only an Unger would do.

The crowd applauded, bringing Binh out of his reverie. Philip, imitating Jason, lay face down as Dia Sobrino's face filled the holo column. Her dark eyes glistened as she imitated Jasmine's facial expressions.

Binh winced at the effort she put into her performance. This was not alien, virginal Cleopatra. There was a look of decadence in Sobrino's face, so unlike the smoothness of faber youth for which Binh had striven.

Jasmine was running through a gracefully executed series of facial expressions, each one surgically and pharmaceutically programmed. The thesp's will was not involved. Like all thesps, she was a biological machine totally controlled by the changes induced by two centuries of dedicated scientists and technicians. Given the intervention of a gifted coach, Jasmine's performance could only be what it was, perfect and fully whole. This was the ultimate justification for the two-hundred-year development of his art.

Yet these professionals, who had devoted their lives to this art, were entranced with Sobrino. They watched her face in total fascination, ignoring Jasmine's subtle movements.

Binh looked away from the holos in anger. He watched M'Wabe hold a lorgnette up to his eyes by its golden stem. The critic smiled as if in rapture. Even this supposed guardian of the highest cultural standards was enchanted by this incompetent performance. What was worse, he thought Binh responsible for this travesty of his production's grand design.

Bianco fidgeted beside him. He understood the gravity of the disruption. Fingering his chin, the assistant avoided Binh's stare, as if to say "What could I have done?"

In the two holo columns, the gestures of Jasmine and Sobrino were roughly synchronized. M'Wabe threw his arm over Binh's shoulders. Binh flinched. The weight of the critic's arm was heavy. M'Wabe's meaty hand squeezed his shoulder tightly.

"It is even more delicious on tape," he said in a stage whisper. Those closest in the crowd, meant to hear this comment, smiled and nodded. The imprimatur had been given.

The heads of Jasmine and Sobrino floated in the holo projection spaces like slowly rotating planets. Binh let his anger pass. Let the two tapes be compared, he thought. The novelty will fade. The sense of an artistic breakthrough will pall. Jasmine's grace will soon make Sobrino's crude performance abhorrent.

The "Inner Tape" jumped. A splice had passed through. Jasmine's looming head faded away. A full view of Jason's body faded in. On the right holo column, Sobrino let a single tear stream down from her left eye. It was a gratuitous and sentimental touch. Tears are purely human, Binh thought. They have no place in an allegory of an alien world.

Jason began a *glissade* as the holo-camera followed. The saurian then executed a spectacular *grand jeté,* following that with another *glissade*. The sequence was an allegory of the human colonist's journey from Earth to Cleopatra.

In the other holo, Sobrino's face disintegrated into a mass of scintillating dots. An image of Philip formed out of the dots; his son began an imitation of the thesp's dance.

If anything, it was more amateurish than Sobrino's performance. Where Jason moved with effortless grace, Philip's leg muscles strained; where Jason's hands conveyed an illusive shift of mood, Philip's hands flapped in random movement.

The technicians—his crew!—began to applaud as Philip departed from Jason's sequence, attempting an inept *pirouette*. It was an indication of how grossly he misinterpreted the spirit of the dance.

Philip had always been impatient with this craft, Binh thought. As a student at the Institute, Philip had rebelled against the study of faber anatomy. He did not take seriously the scientific and technical studies necessary to master the art. For Philip, it was all glamor and flash. Somehow, hard grinding work invalidated it for him.

Binh had always thought his son jealous of the fabers, resenting the talents imbued in them by a sophisticated technology. Now Philip's exhibition was proving him correct.

He has come to drag me down, Binh thought.

M'Wabe's breath wafted against his ear. "This is a stroke of genius, maestro," he whispered. "You have great courage. The thesp/human interface is profound!"

Philip smiled self-consciously as he completed the *pirouette*. Under his leotards his thigh muscles bulged, and he stumbled as he came out of the third turn. Despite this gaucherie, applause erupted from the audience again. All attention was focused on Philip and his great efforting; ignored, the "Inner Tape" ran on, as the thesp executed his dance flawlessly.

Tears welled up in Binh's eyes. Philip and Sobrino

were mocking three months of intense work. The "Inner Tape" was solely his; he had attended to every phase of it from the beginning. He had scoured the thesp markets himself, willing to settle only for perfect specimens. After days of poring over the breeding records, he had discovered Jason and Jasmine.

During their surgical preparation, Binh had stood beside the surgeons as they made the necessary neural modifications. Later, he had stood over the saurians as they awoke. He had been overwhelmed by their beauty. Jason was the most handsome in human terms, with the supple V of his mouth, and the slight suggestion of a human nose. But Jasmine's golden faber eyes had captivated him.

As her anesthetic wore off, her eyelids had fluttered wildly. Despite himself, he had touched her forearm in reassurance. Not that she could ever understand the gesture. After such extensive surgical modification, she was nothing more than *tabula rasa,* an animal which would follow his directions perfectly.

As a student, he had despised such sentimentality. To see a thesp in such a light was a remnant of the Romantic phase which the craft had just outgrown. To give in to such emotions, he had thought, was to go backwards. It was a self-indulgence, foreclosing all possibility of advance in the art.

Binh had been merciless with thesps. If a saurian gave a performance which indicated faulty conditioning or surgical preparation, Binh would immediately halt the taping. Mounting the stage, he would kill the thesp immediately, inserting a stainless steel pick into the brain. It would be as emotionless an act as deleting a mediocre section from a script.

Binh had stopped such practices long ago, but he still had a reputation for ruthlessness. Some of his colleagues would have smiled to see him comforting Jasmine after surgery.

Clashing reds, purples, yellows, and greens, a chaos

of visual noise, pulsed through the left holo, shaking Binh out of his reverie. Startled murmurs filled the hall. Suddenly, the left holo column went milky white. Bursts of red and yellow dots flashed through it at random intervals.

Binh was dizzy from the shock of it: the Inner Tape had been erased. There was no way to recreate it; Jason and Jasmine had been shipped back to the breeder weeks before. By now they had probably been cremated, after bits of their genetic material had been preserved for study. He had put them through well over sixty takes; they had burned out after that.

Binh pushed through the milling crowd, craning his neck for a clear view of the control room. There was a void in his stomach. This was madness. It had to be nothing more than an incredible mistake. One of the junior technicians must have pushed the wrong button. He would have to fire whoever was responsible, assert his authority.

He saw no one in the control room. The hall lights came up and the remaining holo flickered out. M'Wabe rushed up to him, waving frantically. He ignored the critic and looked back up at the control room windows, squinting his eyes against the glare of the hall lights reflecting off the panes.

The lights shone brighter for a moment, and then flickered off. The right holo column rose again. An image of Philip and Sobrino embraced. Their tongues glistened moistly just inside their open mouths. They kissed. The technicians, coaches, journalists, and hangers-on gave them an ovation. Philip and Sobrino slowly twisted down, simulating the act of love.

Binh's lower lip trembled. His son stared down at him through the control room window. A triumphant smile spread across Philip's face. Sobrino came up beside him and looked over the hall impassively.

Overnight, the storm continued. The winds had

shifted to the north, and their velocity had increased. Helicoptering to First City was impossible. Everyone had been forced to spend the night on the island.

Bianco found Binh a room, furnished only with bed and armchair, in a remote public building. Binh left strict orders that he was not to be disturbed. He needed time to think. He found it difficult to believe that Hussein had ordered the tape erased. Hussein was not as mad as that. Open interference with the production would cost him support. It could even jeopardize his control over the Council.

It could only be an aberration, Binh decided, a miscalculation by Sobrino and Philip. He would have to get Philip alone and reason with him. Perhaps something in their failed relationship could be salvaged.

A knock on the door interrupted Binh's musings. M'Wabe's voice hailed him from the corridor. The critic opened the door. Binh, standing by the bed in his red, gold-embroidered nightgown, motioned him inside.

"Bianco insisted I not disturb you, maestro," M'Wabe said, "but I insisted. I take full responsibility."

"This isn't a meeting of the Council, Benito," Binh said irritably. "There's no need for protocol." He stepped away from the bed.

M'Wabe strode across the room, wearing a full, yellow robe which concealed the rotund curves of his body. "It's a matter of great importance," M'Wabe said, coming to a halt by the armchair. "I really feel we should talk, given this evening's happenings."

"You do." Binh turned away and stared at the darkness just outside the room's only window. A tightness formed in his chest. M'Wabe ran his hands lightly over the fabric of the armchair. Binh's chest pain sharpened and localized, just below his left rib cage.

Binh moved closer to the window, breathing shallowly, nursing the pain away. He squinted into the darkness. He could see only rain splattering against the window.

"Maestro, I spoke too soon during the unfortunate."

"Forget it. I have only myself to blame, Benito. I was under the misapprehension that I was in control of the production. The Council obviously has other ideas. You, and the others, continued to give me that impression. To save my feelings, perhaps. I can't blame you for that."

"But maestro, you still have control!" M'Wabe went over to the armchair. In the window, Binh could see him tugging at his robe, as if he had trouble believing it completely covered his body. The critic sat down heavily on the cushions. His face moved into a shadow. "Ah, but I should understand. Self-pity comes easily to faber-masters, especially the greatest ones." The armchair creaked under M'Wabe's weight.

Binh turned away from the window and leaned against the wall. His legs ached, and his forehead was knotted with tension. M'Wabe's words had angered him; he would not let the critic see it in his face.

"Sobrino is dangerous," M'Wabe continued. "You should not underestimate her. Even I have been attracted to her, but my will held me back. But her power is not limitless. Without Hussein she is nothing. And Hussein is changeable. Tomorrow he could deny Sobrino his favor. It is an ambiguous situation."

"You seem particularly sensitive to these subtle shifts of power," Binh said. "You were rather enthusiastic about Sobrino's performance. You thought it a breakthrough, I remember."

"But you misunderstand me!" M'Wabe leaned forward, and his face emerged from the shadow. "The Inner Tape is the finest creation you have ever achieved. I have never moved from that position. Sobrino misinformed me. She said you had authorized the taping."

"Do you still think it a brilliant stroke to merge

the human and the thesp, bring them together in one production?"

M'Wabe was silent for a moment. "Things are changing, maestro," he finally said. "The human must be brought together with the serpent, so to speak. I have not always believed this, but the work of some of the younger avant-gardists has convinced me. I would be less than honest if I said that I was not overjoyed to think you had joined me in that opinion."

"That will never be my intention." Binh raised his voice. "Can't you see what Hussein wants? It should be obvious to you. The young faber-masters are simply playing into the hands of those who would destroy my art. He would destroy the thesps, outlaw their use. Humans would undergo bio-engineering. Who can say what the consequences of that will be?"

"Maestro, I understand your concern. But you must put the problem in perspective."

"You would have me temporize," Binh interrupted, "play the politician."

"But you do not serve your purpose by defiance."

"Benito, their purpose was disruption and nothing more. You read aesthetic motives into their acts where there are none. The intentions of the Council have changed. The ways of my art are no longer politically acceptable." Binh clenched his fists. "But to use my son in this way . . ."

His voice trailed away. His mind was a blank. Staring out the window again, his hands began to tremble. Outside, the darkness was palpable. Despite the thickness of the window pane, he heard the wind moaning against the outer walls of the building. He wanted M'Wabe to leave him alone, but he did not have the courage to tell him. He had to face the fact that he needed this man. Now, with the Inner Tape's erasure, and the sudden appearance of his son, this need was becoming more obvious.

M'Wabe coughed, and began to speak again.

"Maestro, I have always supported you. I remember the first time we met, after I had written about one of your student productions . . ."

"I remember that well, Benito."

". . . and I recall that the particular creation—*The Mask of Socrates* I think you called it—was as controversial in its way as the works coming out of today's avant garde. This fascination with human dancers, with human mime, is spreading among the revolutionary young—it should be nothing new to you, maestro. Our lives have been committed to the nurturing of this difficult art. It is certainly exacting and rewarding to work with thesps, these products of the unique Cleopatran fusion of high technology and art. But you cannot deny the young artist the right to forge new paths."

Binh slammed his fist into his palm. "This is all very well, Benito. I'm sure it will make a stirring article for *The Thespian,* but I am still left with the wreckage of my production. And to have my son . . ." He could not speak the words.

M'Wabe stared impassively, waiting for him to continue.

"You must understand the implications," Binh said after a moment. "If this woman Sobrino can invade my set— I felt like strangling them both. If she weren't Hussein's representative . . ."

M'Wabe stood up with a grunt. He blinked his eyes shut and smiled, as if he were listening to an inner voice.

"You were wise to restrain yourself. It must have been a great effort after such provocation. But surely you can piece something together from the outtakes? Failing that, other thesps can be procured. After all, Hussein has agreed to extend the production's financing over the original budget—which, you must remember, you have run through already. The Inner Tape can still be shot."

M'Wabe stared at him sharply for a moment. He

moved toward the door. A sudden realization chilled Binh. He turned away from M'Wabe. If his expression had changed, he could not let the critic see it.

It was so obvious—why had he not seen it from the first? M'Wabe was not representing himself. He was serving Hussein's interests. Hussein had decided that Binh could no longer be trusted with complete authority of the production. Politically, there was too much at stake. M'Wabe had been sent here to keep him within bounds. The critic had done his first job well—the Inner Tape had been erased. Binh had been kept from confronting Sobrino and his son. They had taken the source of his creativity, his self-control, very much for granted. Now the parameters of the game had been changed. The new ground rules had to be explained. Who better to explain them than Benito M'Wabe, his old friend, his confidant, his supporter?

Binh glanced around after a moment. M'Wabe was standing silently by the door.

"So it should be clear, maestro," M'Wabe said quietly, "nothing is irreparable. Hussein's financing is unlimited, for all practical purposes. For patriotic reasons, he had a great interest in this production. Let him serve you."

M'Wabe opened the door and waited for a moment. It was as if he expected Binh to make a reply. After a few moments of silence, the critic shrugged and walked out into the hall.

"The situation should be seen clearly, maestro," M'Wabe said, turning. "Your son and this young woman are impetuous, as we were. All your artistic intentions can still be fulfilled. Politically, however, some cosmetics are in order."

M'Wabe walked down the hallway, leaving the door open. A bright shaft of yellow light streamed into the room. Moving slowly across the room, Binh pushed the door shut. He stared through the storm-battered window. Outside, the darkness gathered thickly, as if its weight would break through the glass and engulf him.

Binh dreamt himself a young man again, a student. Somehow he had lost his way in a rainstorm. He came upon his teacher's home, a large stone house surrounded by gardens. It rained harder, until he was soaked to the skin. There was no answer. He had an image in his mind of his teacher lurking behind the walls, angry with him over an imagined slight, set on teaching him a lesson by refusing to come to the door.

He heard a stirring behind the door. He shouted out, and thunder rumbled. Suddenly he panicked. Something nameless stalked him. Only by entering the house could he escape it. He shouted his teacher's name. A face appeared at the window in the middle of the door. It was not his teacher. It was a face without features, a blank surface of flesh confronting him, unable to gesture, unable to speak.

Binh jolted awake. Caesar's harsh light glared through the window, forcing him to close his eyes again. The light tinged his eyelids a brilliant orange. A dull pain throbbed behind his eyes.

He sat on the edge of the bed, shivering with uneasiness. Binh could usually sense the meaning of a dream, but the significance of this nightmare escaped him. Why had he dreamed of his teacher? It was so long ago; he had forgotten the man's name. He had learned meditation from this man, one of the required courses at the institute, but he had never regarded it as a technique by which mystical truths would be revealed. He had not formed a devotion to the teacher as so many others had done. By practicing his own art he would find whatever truths he would find. Meditation was simply a way to ease his mind and body out of the torment of overwork.

Binh dressed and left the room. Walking on the beach, he watched Caesar rise above the water. It was still less than an hour after daybreak. Sectos swarmed in the humid morning air, feeding on the detritus of the sea.

Binh eased his way along the side of a dune. A cloud of smidgens flew at his face. He waved his arms to fend them off. In spring, these sectos were common at this latitude; Binh was particularly sensitive to their bite.

Beyond the dunes, the beach was level. Binh walked slowly toward the sea. His head still throbbed, and his muscles were unusually stiff. Images from the last twenty-four hours swirled chaotically in his mind. He tried to think of ways to salvage something from yesterday's wreckage, but there were no easy solutions.

There were no facilities for boarding thesps on the island. Every saurian had to be brought over from First City for a day's shooting. The week's storms had forced him to use every available thesp. Those who had performed during the week had all been exhausted.

Work would have to be suspended while the markets were searched. It would not be easy. Bianco would have to go himself. He would have to pass on the saurians. To make matters worse, this was the height of the production season. There was no guarantee a suitable pair could be found. The production might have to be terminated indefinitely.

There was one other option, but he had no confidence in it. The outtakes could be edited, as M'Wabe had suggested. Something like the erased Inner Tape could be constructed. But it would be a compromise, nothing more. Binh watched the sea ripple slowly to the shore. It might be the only course he had left.

Halfway to the water's edge, Binh stopped. It was too early for most of the journalists, but some of them might be awake in hopes of getting transportation back to First City. He did not want to face them after last night. The dunes behind him were the only protection he would have on the beach. Despite this headache, he hurried back toward them.

Between the dunes, plant life imported from Earth by

legions of immigrants co-existed with the flora of Cleopatra. Ordinary Earth grasses flourished on the rich nutrients beneath the thin layer of sand. Binh gingerly stepped over a growth of grenade plants as he skirted the side of a dune. The plants were harmless, but they were prone to explode without warning, sending their prickly seeds flying in all directions. Here and there, civic groups had planted several varieties of Earth flowers. Roses, begonias, and morning glories grew in beds of rich topsoil, providing displays of color. It was as if the strange and beautiful pseudoblooms of the Cleopatran tropics were not lovely enough, as if the human settlers of Cleopatra still needed ties to the teeming, tormented globe they had left behind, even if those ties were as tenuous as flowers.

Thoughts raced through Binh's mind. Every one brought him back to the problem of his production. He should never have taken the commission, he thought. But he had gone through some dry years. Funding and ideas had simultaneously dried up. Binh stopped, watching a cloud of smidgens skim the crest of a dune. Perhaps it had been because he had lied to himself, and had forgotten that lies were death to his art. Perhaps he had lost the youthful vigor of his talent because he had found it possible to cut off all ties to his family without any sense of loss.

Only something less than a human being would find that possible, Binh thought. How long ago had Anna died? Thirteen years? Fourteen? How long had it been since he had a conversation with Philip? He had always thought that his personal life had simply happened to him. But how much of it was really his responsibility?

Anna had worked for him as a coach after their graduation from the institute. Binh had suspected her of envying the thesps. At the Institute, she had been the best dance student, but she had only been able to use that talent as a coach. It was strange, as if Philip had carried that longing into the present.

Binh's relationship with Anna had not been smooth. For the two years they were together, they had fought continuously. On the surface, the arguments were over artistic matters. Binh often accused her of wanting control, of desiring to supplant him as the final authority on the set. He now could understand how stupid he had been. She had wanted nothing more than his respect. For all these years Binh had blamed himself for not showing her his concern.

The police had discovered her dead one morning. Her head had been smashed, and she had lain in a First City alley for over a day. Just one more meaningless death in the jungle of First City. Aside from the uneasy political conditions, which had spawned civil unrest for most of Binh's life, all urban areas on Cleopatra were the setting of random violence. It was as if the cities themselves periodically rose up to destroy one of their own, and were slowly suiciding, unable to reconcile themselves to their human mass.

Anna's death had also murdered his relationship with Philip. As an eight-year-old, his son had idolized him. Philip had openly proclaimed his intention of following his father's career. But Anna's absurd death had ended all communication between them. Philip had retreated into a passivity and silence which years of psychiatric treatment could not break.

When Philip turned eighteen, he had begun a public rebellion against him. He wrote denunciations of his father's work, publishing them in the journals of obscure political cults. Philip then had joined one movement after another, all of which espoused insanely destructive ideologies.

Musing, Binh walked halfway around the island. He reached an area beyond the dunes. A cold wind blasted his face. From this vantage point, he had an unimpeded view of First City. At a distance of more than eight kilometers the city seemed a natural object, its spires and waterfront a crystalline growth. In this perfect weather, so unusual in a Cleopatran spring, the city's smog had been blown away. Every detail of its architecture was visible. Caesar glinted off the silver tops of the government buildings. Binh began to think it was possible to see his own house, high on top of the hills beyond the city.

He had spent his entire life within fifty miles of First City. There had been no reason to travel anywhere else. The holos brought him all the sights of Cleopatra. He had always had everything he needed; his career had always been more than adequately nurtured. Why then did he feel so limited, so hopeless now, staring at this great city which commemorated a great human hegira, an escape from a dying world.

He walked over to a telescope, permanently mounted for the tourists who usually swarmed over the island. Pointing it across the channel, he saw ships entering the harbor, moving toward the docks. He could see the urban transports swooshing through their clear, suspended tubes. Turning up the magnification, he saw people at the windows of office buildings, shuffling papers, staring out at this beautiful harbor.

Binh swung the instrument around, panning it over the beach. Foreshortened by the telescope's optics, the waves hitting the beach seemed larger, more threatening, as if a storm were building. A faber appeared in his line of sight, one of the many allowed to remain on the island to give the appearance that the site of the first human touchdown remained in its natural state. Binh could not be sure whether the saurian was a male or female. It squatted by the shore, scooping up clumps of sea grass and stuffing them in its mouth.

A shout startled him. Binh turned from the telescope. In the distance, two figures were running down the beach toward the faber, who continued to feed itself. Looking through the telescope, Binh saw Philip and Sobrino. They shouted, as if to drive the saurian away from the surf.

Sobrino was holding what appeared to be a weapon. She waved it threateningly in the faber's direction. Binh could now see the saurian clearly. It was a female, with a prominent crest. The faber glanced up, her tongue flashing about within her V-shaped mouth, swallowing the remains of the sea grass, golden eyes wide.

Sobrino stared at the faber in disgust. Philip, his face more wrinkled than Binh remembered, kept staring at Sobrino, as if something in her face fascinated him.

Binh could not keep his eyes away from the woman's body. She wore a black leather jump suit. It was decorated with silver ornaments running along her pelvis, breast, and thighs. Again, Binh was struck by her raw sexuality. She moved easily; there was no flab on her well-muscled body. As she lifted the weapon-like object in her hand, her breasts rose, stretching the leather drawn tightly over their firmness.

He recognized the object—it was a sounder, which emitted a raucous blast extremely unpleasant to the fabers. He had sometimes used it himself, when preparing thesps for taping. With it he could get their immediate attention, and it made the saurians more manageable afterwards.

Sobrino flicked her wrists. The grinding whine of the sounder blared out, overriding the roar of the surf. The faber, totally confused, began running into the water, turning and splashing back toward the beach as the sound continued. Reaching the beach, the saurian fell on her stomach, digging into the sand with her claws.

This was a new kind of sounder, Binh realized. The blast was more intense, and the faber was reacting unusually. Her legs twitched in spasms. Thrashing about on her side, her body trembled violently. Her head hung loosely to the side, as if it had been broken. As her eyes rolled back white in her eye sockets, she vomited a yellow liquid which was rapidly absorbed by the sand.

Binh took his eyes away from the telescope, shouted his son's name, and ran toward the helpless faber, who was more than sixty meters away. Halfway there, his foot sank into a spot of soft sand and he stumbled. When he got to his feet again, Philip and Sobrino had disappeared. The faber still shook by the water's edge.

He reached the saurian and knelt beside her. By this time the spasms had lessened. The faber's eyes darted normally back and forth. Binh rose to his feet. The beach was empty. He kicked the sand in anger, startling the faber. She uttered a thin, high-pitched sound and bounded off, disappearing into the dunes.

Binh heard laughter. Philip and Sobrino stood a few meters away. Philip had his arm around her broad shoulders. He flashed a smile and revealed a mouthful of broken teeth. The political riots had taken their toll on him.

"Hello, Father dear, Maestro Binh," Philip said.

Sobrino laughed. Her eyes were blank, empty of sparkle. She looked through him as if he were the open sea, or an arid stretch of sand.

"I want to talk to you, Philip," he said. "I was surprised to see you last night."

"I'd say so," Sobrino said, "to judge by your expression when the holo . . ." She made a wiping motion with her hands.

Anger made him tense his jaw. "You admit . . ."

"Exactly nothing, maestro. Isn't that what they call you?" She moved closer. She looked at Binh with contempt. Turning to Philip, she said "Isn't that what they call your famous father, Philip?"

"Who gave you authorization to visit the set last night? Who allowed you access to the taping facilities?" Binh raised his voice.

Sobrino ran the tip of her index finger lightly over the nape of Philip's neck. "Who indeed?" she said, as if musing to herself.

Philip laughed. "You must know who we represent."

Sobrino nuzzled the side of Philip's head. "Of course he does," she said. "Every faber-master knows the source of his funding, unless they choose to lie to themselves. Isn't that so, Maestro Binh?"

Binh was overcome by vertigo. He could not close his eyes and wait until it passed. He could not betray weakness. He looked at the sea.

"I'm sure you will have no objection, Maestro," Sobrino said, "to our continued presence on the set. Isn't that right? That is, if you want things to continue as they have been."

Binh said nothing as he continued looking out to sea.

"I'm sure the name Kevin Hussein means a great deal to you," she said, as she and Philip began to walk away. "Soon his name will have greater meaning to all the peoples of Cleopatra."

Binh watched them stroll slowly toward the dunes. The vertigo was quite strong now. He could think of nothing but the way the waves now moved slowly toward the shore, the way the faber had not waited for him to bend down and offer his sympathy.

Overnight, Bianco had miraculously procured two first-rate thesps, a male Resnick and a female Unger. They had been bred and designed to react predictably to the same coaching, whether the technique was imitative, surgical intervention, or a combination of the two. Bianco claimed they were better than Jason and Jasmine. The Inner Tape, he said, could be reproduced in only one or two takes.

A new set had been erected in the public hall. When Binh arrived, his crew was already working. The thesps had been nicknamed Scylla and Charybdis by some comedian on the crew. Since they had been surgically prepared before coming to the island, Binh had only to give them their final coaching.

It could have been worse. Only an hour of the Inner Tape had been erased. Most of it had been a single sequence intended to intercut with other improvisations, which had all been taped long ago.

Binh approached the thesps, who were slumped against a wall in the coaching area. He began to feel hopeful. They appeared to be prime specimens, and bore a striking resemblance to Jason and Jasmine.

Binh had induced a light state of hypnosis in both thesps, and was beginning to suggest movements for the first part of the sequence, when Bianco rushed over.

"There's nothing I could do," he said in agitation. "Sobrino insisted. She said you talked to her on the beach yesterday. She said she understood the situation perfectly. She wants to watch the taping from the control room."

Hussein is tightening his control, Binh thought. There was nothing he could do. He continued his work on the male thesp.

"Forget her," he blurted out in irritation. "We have more important things to think about."

Despite the quality of the thesps, the coaching took longer than Binh had anticipated. He called Osbeck over to assist. While Bianco co-ordinated the technicians in the control room and on the production floor, Binh and Osbeck danced the final sequences for Scylla and Charybdis.

The crew kept the journalists and other spectators back from the main taping area, which was a circular stage surrounded by a light, azure backdrop. Binh and Osbeck led the thesps onto the stage, showing them their beginning positions. As the camera crews completed their preparations, Binh made tests on the thesps, making sure the dances had been learned.

This portion was the death sequence. Running through it in his mind. Binh took a grim satisfaction from the spare, arid hopelessness of the plot. Some scientists had called the fabers a doomed race. Even if man had not colonized Cleopatra, the saurians' lack of a social fabric and intelligence would eventually lead to their extinction. This dance sequence dramatized that theory; in it, Scylla and Charybdis would act out a dance of death. It was a theme repeated throughout the production.

Binh completed his work and left the stage. M'Wabe walked over to him. The critic looked at the thesps, who waited impassively in their positions. A slight smile came to M'Wabe's lips.

"I told Sobrino you were capable of seeing this situation with great clarity, maestro. Things should go well now."

Binh nodded abstractly. M'Wabe was lost to him.

I walk a tightrope, Binh thought. He could only see the production to the end if he avoided any innovation, any deviation from the script of the Inner Tape.

He called for silence. The holo-cameras began to hum. Osbeck gave the thesps the starting stimulus; they moved into their *danse macabre*. Binh's hands began to tremble.

It was done in less than fifteen minutes. The public hall, quiet for the taping, suddenly resounded with applause. Sobrino appeared in the midst of the crowd. Everyone gave her space, as if she were the object of the ovation. Philip was not with her.

"We are the only thing standing between the fabers and extinction," she said in a loud, declaiming voice.

Binh winced as the crowd fell silent. This was dogma right out of a Scientific Transcendence propaganda leaflet, injected now to dilute the richness of the scene he had just taped, reducing it to a gloss on the wisdom of Kevin Hussein.

"Maestro Binh," Sobrino said. "This dance was good, surprisingly so. I'm sure Kevin Hussein would approve of its message wholeheartedly. But one thing troubles me, and I'm sure it would distress Mr. Hussein if he were here."

"I think I see what you mean," Benito M'Wabe said, simpering. He pushed his way to the front of the crowd. "The *danse macabre* cries out for the human element. The audience will hunger for the knowledge that humanity, the conquerer of Cleopatra, had overcome the animalism which could drive the fabers into extinction."

"*Will* drive them into extinction, M'Wabe," Sobrino interjected. "They have given us sufficient lessons in baseness. I, for one, would be happy to watch the last faber die."

I am losing control, Binh thought. He had never allowed aesthetic or ideological discussions in the middle of a production. Now as this prattle went on, the crew stopped their work to listen, and the energy needed to finish the taping was being deflected.

Binh motioned rudely to a technician who was leaning against a holo-camera. "Set up for the next sequence," he ordered.

"Ah," laughed Sobrino. M'Wabe smiled weakly beside her. "Maestro Binh will not allow his work to be questioned. Perhaps when the production is complete, when he has used the people's wealth for his own purposes, the maestro will consent to be praised."

"You have no right to interrupt our work," Binh shouted. "You are here only as an observer."

" 'Our work,' the maestro says." Sobrino turned to address the crowd. "The maestro will restrict me while he can." She glared at Binh. "At this moment, there is nothing standing in your way, Maestro Binh. But nothing goes unnoticed. So far you haven't broken any guidelines."

"To hell with your guidelines!" Binh exploded. The crew looked at him in shock. He rarely threw tantrums on the set. Binh no longer cared what anyone thought. His anger made him giddy.

He motioned at Bianco. The assistant hesitated, but finally walked toward him.

"Clear the set!" Binh ordered.

Sobrino gave him a mock bow. "But of course, maestro. By all means, exercise your authority." She whirled around and pushed through the crowd.

The journalists, hoping for more fireworks, objected. Binh knew this was the story they had been sent here to get.

He slumped into a canvas-backed chair. His body prickled with numbness; he could not concentrate on the script pages he held in his hands. Across the hall, M'Wabe stared at him with an ambiguous expression.

Binh looked away. M'Wabe was their puppet now. On the stage, Scylla and Charybdis held their final positions; no one had given them the signal to rest. The female sprawled on the floor like a corpse. The male held his claws to his face as if he were just about to rip the eyes out of his head.

Binh sat watching them. Somehow, the tableau was comforting.

"You must understand, maestro," M'Wabe said. "Your production has impinged on certain political realities."

Binh had been preparing to sleep when the critic came up to his room. A storm had blown in, blocking all travel to First City. M'Wabe was clearly restless. The wrinkles on his brow deepened as he paced the floor at the foot of Binh's bed.

"I'm aware of certain pressures, Benito," A pain stabbed his chest. Watching M'Wabe pace, Binh breathed shallowly.

The critic stared at him in open disbelief. "You do yourself an injustice by being so blasé about them. You have a gift, a gift you can give to the people of Cleopatra. The planet is about to come apart. In the southern hemisphere, certain groups are already openly defying the Council. They are in the process of splitting away from the planetary government. These people represent ideologies of the most retrograde variety."

"I fail to see the relevance. I have my work to complete."

"The completion of your work depends on your

political sophistication." He glared at Binh balefully. "You are in the eye of the hurricane. In some ways you have always been—it is in the nature of your art, a part of being an artist. It is a problem I will never face. But to foolishly throw everything away, out of the most childish kind of naiveté . . ."

"It's not your place, Benito, to instruct me in politics. There are enough buffoons like Hussein on Cleopatra."

"I'm afraid it's necessary to give you a civics lesson, maestro, since you persist in this suicidal thinking. I know it is difficult to understand the importance of political struggles unless they impinge on our lives directly, but it is folly to ignore them when they do."

"I've lost family in political riots, Benito. I have been a participant."

M'Wabe laughed dryly. "There are few of our class who haven't been. I was with my wife when she died in a riot, and was injured myself. It was five years ago." He made a fist and held it in front of his chest, turning it over slowly, as if some message could be read there. "Forgive my seeming indifference, maestro, but your career has not been impeded. Neither was mine. The political events of the last twenty-five years have given you an environment in which you have influence and power, whether you choose to face that fact or not.

"Now your career is in jeopardy. When the Council held the purse strings for the production, you were free. You could have justified anything in the name of planetary unity, since that was the theme of your commission. But Hussein is now the deciding voice on the Council. The various dissenting groups in the southern hemisphere and the wild men in Pindaria all may be more radical than he, but they will temporize as long as they perceive him as having final power. The forces which advocate turning Cleopatra into a replica of Earth, preserving only small portions of the surface in their natural state, support him, even though he does not totally agree with their positions. He may be this planet's last hope, the only means through which we can preserve a planetary government."

M'Wabe paused, as if he expected a reply. Binh said nothing.

"Then do you see," M'Wabe said after a moment, "that you will have to bend? I want your career to survive. When Sobrino is on the set, you will have to bow to at least one or two of her demands."

"In other words, I should cede to her some of my artistic control."

"This attitude of your is precisely the trouble. You're playing by the old rules. You can have artistic autonomy only as long as you make them believe they have final say over you. You are subtle enough to have your own way, and theirs as well."

"I'm sure you have the requisite subtlety, Benito." Binh got out of bed, draped a robe around his shoulders, and slowly walked to the window. The storm had ended. Wind was blowing rivulets of water down the pane.

"Is Sobrino making objections to the entire production," he asked, "or just to portions? I'm sure someone has been running them for her. Perhaps it was you, Benito."

"Surely, maestro," M'Wabe began in a conciliatory tone, "you can see she is an ideological primitive?"

"What changes does she want?"

"They ask to insert a minor segment, nothing more. They have to save face, don't you see?"

"I don't give a damn about their political image!" Binh picked up a script of the production off the bedstand. He held it up for M'Wabe to see. "Do you see this, Benito? Do you understand what it means to me. You of all people should understand that this production is all of a piece. Their tampering would destroy it totally."

"I have never seen such a lack of self-interest,"

M'Wabe said, laughing as if in disbelief. "What exactly do you think your position is? Twenty-five years ago we both fought to restrict bio-engineering to fabers. We were misled by our youthful idealism. It was a self-serving political position, maestro. We joined forces with the most ignorant and reactionary groups on Cleopatra to promote our own ends. How sincere were we, maestro? Were we really so concerned about the human race? Or was it our careers that drove us into the streets? It is painful to reconsider the idealism of youth, but perhaps we should begin."

"What kind of segment do they want?"

M'Wabe sat in the armchair. "Just one segment featuring human dancers."

"That would be Philip and Sobrino?"

"Precisely."

Binh moved away from the window. He remembered bringing Philip to the set of *The Untold Want*. It had been only months after Anna's death. Binh had thought the visit would bring him closer to his son, who had already sunk deeply into passivity. Watching the thesps dance, Philip's eyes had brightened. Something had taken up Binh's attention, and he had had to leave his son alone. Later, when the day's taping had finished, Binh could not find Philip anywhere. One of the technicians finally had found him in an unused store room. Under a bare light bulb, Philip was imitating the dances he had seen earlier in the day. Standing in the door, Binh had laughed as his son attempted to *pirouette*. Philip first had looked at him with an embarrassed expression. Then his eyes had gone blank again.

"So you are their spokesman, then," Binh said.

M'Wabe looked at him pleadingly. "Not theirs, maestro, yours. And mine. Without this art, our lives amount to nothing. Unless we compromise now, in a few years this craft will be an antique, a memento of a vaguely remembered decadence. It will be replaced by sterner, more socially useful forms. We have got to try and make our peace with them now, maestro. They may not offer us this opportunity again."

Binh sat down on the edge of the bed. He put his head down, letting his arms hang loosely at his sides. His body felt drained. He wanted to speak words which would save them both.

"Benito, I cannot. You know that."

"Maestro . . ." M'Wabe's voice trailed off. He spread his hands out imploringly.

"Perhaps you should not call me 'maestro'."

M'Wabe rose abruptly and left the room. Binh sat motionless, listening to the critic's footsteps fading down the hall.

Charybdis lay unconscious on a platform at the center of the stage. Bending over him, Binh held the syringe just above the thesp's scalp. An amber drop glistened on the needle's tip.

There was little time. If he waited out the night, this scene would never be taped. It would have to be done now, while the equipment was still in place. Now he could act without considering the consequences.

Binh stared at the six-digit breeding number tattooed in red behind the thesp's right ear. Beneath tightly closed eyelids, the saurian's eyes fluttered in dream sleep. The first injections were taking hold. Binh felt the thesp's pulse, then pierced its scalp with the syringe, depressing the plunger quickly.

Binh ran his eyes over the scales on the saurian's green chest. Charybdis was beautiful, absolute perfection. He studied the serene face. It could have been a death mask.

He felt the sutures on the thesp's scalp. Charybdis had undergone surgery only days before. The incision had just begun to heal. No matter. He covered it with make-up; the holo-cameras would not pick it up.

The cortizine injection had immediate effect. Binh looked at his watch; he only had the rest of the night at best. Charybdis's eyes fluttered open and stared up blankly. The drug would give the saurian the extra strength he would need for the dance. Without it, after the tapings of the afternoon, he would find the steps impossible to execute. The thesp would have to be destroyed after the taping, even with the drug.

Binh helped Charybdis stand. The saurian's body was hard with muscle, but it limply yielded to his direction, standing straight at the center of the stage while Binh walked slowly backwards, studying the thesp's position.

Bianco's voice came over the public address system.

"The control room is empty. I couldn't convince any technicians to come. Maestro, it's past four in the morning."

Binh had expected that. He was now on the losing side in the game. The technicians were looking after themselves. Only Bianco was foolish enough to be loyal.

Binh picked up an intercom microphone. "Then run the equipment. I've already set up the cameras. They can be operated from the control room."

"What if we have to do another take? You'll need me on the floor."

"It won't be necessary," Binh said quietly. Besides, he thought, Bianco would be safer in the control room if they should be interrupted.

This will be a free dance, Binh thought. He dropped the microphone to signal the conversation was at an end. The drugs and surgery would contribute to a gentle beginning. The thought encouraged him; it would be comforting to watch solitary grace. Then at the proper moment, when it would seem the thesp could dance forever, Binh would introduce jarring stimuli, and the saurian would follow its programming. Binh wanted a simulation of death; it would go beyond the *danse macabre* he had taped earlier in the day.

"Maestro!" Bianco shouted over the loudspeakers. Feedback echoed through the hall.

Binh looked up at the control room. Bianco stood with his back to the window, confronting four armed men. They wore the black uniform of Kevin Hussein's private guards.

Something slammed behind him. He turned to see the hall's double doors swing open. Dia Sobrino strode through, surrounded by another force of armed men. On her signal, they quickly encircled the stage and began to smash the holo-cameras with their rifle butts.

Binh cried out and lunged at a burly guard. The man swung the other end of the rifle around, hitting Binh on the side of the head. The hall dissolved away as Binh fell back.

They slapped him back into consciousness. Binh brought his hand up to the side of his head to fend off the blows. His hair was caked with dried blood.

He was slumped in the back of a windowless van. His head lay against the cold metal surface of a wheel hump. The wheel hit a bump. Something sharp jabbed the back of his head.

The guards squatted on either side of him, clutching automatic rifles. Binh's eyes ran over the surface markings of a weapon as he began to slip back into unconsciousness. A guard grabbed his shoulder and shook him awake.

The van screeched to a stop. The loading gate was swung down, and a guard pushed Binh toward it with the muzzle of his weapon.

Outside, they escorted him over the glare of white pavement, toward a group of grey, reinforced concrete domes. It is Kevin Hussein's villa, Binh thought. He had seen pictures of it in some propaganda leaflets.

They reached the largest dome. Inside, the guards pushed Binh ahead of them, ordering him to walk into a long, empty tunnel. After walking a few minutes, Binh heard the dim sounds of a crowd reverberating along the curving walls.

"Run!" A guard behind him ordered. "Run, or I'll smash your head open!"

Binh ran, but after a few meters pain shot through his left knee, and his leg collapsed. As he sprawled on the floor, a rifle butt smashed into the small of his back.

"Get up!" a guard shouted, kicking him in the side. Trying to protect himself, Binh rolled into a ball.

A shouting crowd rushed down the tunnel and surrounded him. They picked Binh up roughly and carried him into a fluorescent lighted hall. Held up in the midst of a press of people, Binh could see nothing but the intricate lacing supports etched into the hall's immense dome.

"Bring him up on stage!" Dia Sobrino's voice sounded over loudspeakers. They carried him up, dropping him on a hardwood surface. Then they withdrew as quickly as they had surrounded him. Overhead, a bank of lights glared down at him.

Binh slowly stood up. Standing unsteadily on aching legs, he seemed to be alone, encircled by walls of light. The crowd burst into applause. Dia Sobrino walked across the stage toward him, followed by two guards who pushed Scylla and Charybdis before them.

Sobrino stood beside Binh, her hands hanging limply at her side. The crowd became silent.

"Thank you," she said to them. "I'm glad you could be here. You will all find this little performance quite instructive, I'm sure. You all recognize Marcus Binh."

The crowd howled, shouting insults. Something hurtled toward him out of the glare and smashed at his feet.

"Silence!" Sobrino commanded, holding up her arms. "We have much to do. This man's name is known throughout Cleopatra. After tonight he will be known for what he really is, a traitor, a man who would hold the benefits of science back from the peoples of Cleopatra."

The crowd began shouting insults again. More objects were thrown on stage. Binh, holding his hand against the light, moved back uncertainly as objects fell around him.

"Binh represents everything we are fighting against," she continued. "He fought to deny us the fruits of science when the Council was overthrown, and the repressive laws against bio-engineering were imposed upon us. What was his purpose? Whose interests did he serve? Only his own interests, and the interests of his elitist friends. Now we will see the product of Marcus Binh's philosophy. Here is his contribution to human progress."

Sobrino turned to the back of the stage. "Bring them on!" she shouted. "Now you will see how Binh was using the Council's money, your money."

The guards prodded the thesps with their rifles. As the crowd shouted derisively, Scylla and Charybdis stumbled forward. After moving a few meters, they came to a halt and stood slumping, their heads tilted.

"Is this all?" Sobrino shouted at Binh. "Don't they have a dance for us?"

The crowd fell silent. Binh stared at Sobrino and said nothing.

A guard pressed the muzzle of a rifle against his temple.

"Please, maestro, give them their signal. Surely they must have some steps. After all, you were just about to tape when we invited you to visit us."

Binh stared at Sobrino in despair. Charybdis was ready to perform, but Scylla was weak. He had planned to ship her back to market, where she would probably be terminated. If he let her dance with Charybdis, the combination of grace and awkwardness would certainly inflame the crowd.

The guard pressed the muzzle against his skull. The crowd erupted in catcalls again. Binh commanded the thesps to dance.

Charybdis began a *glissade,* circling Scylla. The female began a halting *pirouette,* but she could not complete it. She fell to the stage, her breath rasping. Charybdis continued to *glissade* around her, as if she were some kind of prey.

The crowd's shouting grew to a roar. Sobrino motined them to be quiet.

"Would you agree that the female is burned out, maestro? Isn't that the jargon?" she asked. "Well, do what has to be done, Maestro Binh. One cannot be sentimental about a thesp, after all."

She motioned to a guard, who put a wooden-handled, stainless steel pick into Binh's hands.

The crowd's shouting became a massive physical presence, coming in like a wave out of the glare just beyond the end of the stage. Binh turned and ran to the rear of the stage. Throwing the pick away, he pressed himself against the wall.

The screams sounded closer. Three guards surrounded him. People were charging through the glare. They encircled the thesps and pummeled them to the floor.

"We'll do it for you, maestro," Sobrino shouted. "Understand what this makes you!"

Binh screamed and tried to run toward the thesps. The guards grabbed his arms and held him back. The mob beat the thesps with wooden sticks. Scylla and Charybdis twitched on the stage. Binh saw a pink rivulet of blood coursing from the corner of the male's mouth.

Sobrino stood before him, her hands on her hips, blocking his view of the beating. Her eyes flashed as she raised her hand to point at Binh. The guards shoved him forward.

Binh fell to the floor. A guard held him down while Sobrino prepared a syringe.

"We have a place for you at Camp Isolation, maestro," she said, shoving the syringe into his arm. "There you might be able to put your talents to some social use."

Binh felt himself sinking into darkness. He gazed impassively at the crumpled bodies of Scylla and Charybdis as his heavy lids closed.

Binh awoke, jarred by an uneven pitching motion. For an instant, he stared at Caesar's brilliance through a clear dome. An afterimage spread out at the center of his vision when he turned away and blinked. Suddenly, he pitched forward as the floor moved again, and he was pressed against a curved wall.

Binh tried to stand, but a searing pain in his knee forced him into a prone position. He thought of Scylla and Charybdis, their brutal death. The afterimage floated everywhere he looked, as if it were a bubble rising up slowly beneath the sea.

He suddenly became nauseated. Binh stared at his pale, trembling hand lying across a riveted metal surface. He could have been anywhere, contained even in an open storage tank. But he could hear faint whirrings. The floor vibrated rhythmically beneath him. He was in a ship of some kind, but not a land car. The motions were fluid. He thought of floating on a choppy sea, and his nausea overwhelmed him. He vomited after a sudden jolt threw him forward again.

A grinding sound shuddered through the metallic surfaces. Somewhere above him, machinery whined. Then there was silence. Binh lay still, aching with fatigue.

He closed his eyes, and opened them. Hours had passed. The afterimage had disappeared, and a dim light glimmered. Somehow, he managed to stand. His legs ached with numbness. He rubbed them back to life for a moment before he realized where he was.

He had been packed aboard an air car. The guards had thrown him into a rear compartment. He tried the door, but it was locked. Binh wondered how many of the guards had come along. I am going to die, he thought. He tried to remember what Sobrino had said before the drug had overwhelmed him, but he could only recall the needle's sting as it slid into his arm, and Sobrino standing over him, smiling.

The air car rocked forward and dived. Binh was

thrown back, hitting his shoulder against the wall. He dragged himself into the seat, and buckled the seat belt.

The world exploded, and his vision went red.

When Binh opened his eyes a dim light shone through the overhead dome. Smoke filled the passenger compartment. A warning buzzer shattered his ears. The ship had held together, but it was now on fire. Binh unbuckled the belt and rushed for the door, which had been twisted open by the crash.

Seeing open sky, Binh jumped. He fell to the rocky sand, bruising his hip. A loud hissing erupted behind him; he thought of a fuel line spewing out on hot metal.

His knee throbbed as he crawled away from the air car. The dry desert air seared his lungs as he pulled his body over the rocks. He turned around and looked at the air car. The pilot's head was scarlet against the cockpit windshield.

A concussion threw him against the side of an outcropping. He felt a scorching heat against his back. The air car was an orange ball of flame.

Binh walked. There was nothing else to do. He gauged the direction by the position of Caesar in the sky. His body trembled violently, but his mind was beginning to clear.

Sobrino had mentioned Camp Isolation. Binh had read about the place in some Council factsheet. It was an experimental bio-engineering station.

Binh shook his head; confusion clouded his mind again. What did Hussein and his cult have to do with Camp Isolation? Perhaps Hussein's control of the Council was now absolute, and the camp was being readied for a changeover to human experimentation.

If so, Binh thought, I would make an unlikely candidate. He kept walking. Whatever went on there, Camp Isolation was his only chance. By his estimation, he was walking south. The Isolation Mountains were visible on the horizon. The camp was in the foothills.

Binh's legs gave out as evening approached. His stomach was aflame. Sitting against a rock, he chewed on a piece of cactusspur. Its bitter moisture stung his throat.

Binh slept. In the morning, the chittering of fabers awoke him. A broad-chested saurian stood ten meters away, tearing flesh from a fresh carcass. The horizon was an orange glow. Stuffing a piece of meat in his mouth, the faber stared at Binh with golden eyes.

The carcass was a king gator. The skull was bashed in. Binh could not understand how the solitary faber had managed that. He staggered to his feet and leaned against a rock. Dizziness seized him. He would let the desert take him now. Above and behind him, he heard more chittering, and the sounds of pebbles falling. Three fabers stood widely apart, watching the hunter feast upon the kill. After he was bloated, they would go down one by one and take what they needed.

Binh stared at the mountains. Floating just above the desert sand, he saw buildings shimmering. He blinked his eyes, and the mirage disappeared.

He pushed his body away from the rock, staggering toward the faber and his carcass. The waiting fabers chittered loudly while the hunter squatted and watched him for a moment before slowly moving away.

Camp Isolation shimmered in the distance. He saw a line of fabers in khaki battle fatigues marching toward the mountains. A black-uniformed guard trotted beside them; his *hup, hup, hup* was loud in the stillness of the desert.

Binh followed them, walking toward the peaks.

2553 A.D.

The emerging nations drifted apart in their outlooks. There were small wars and large wars . . .

A small nation, Casca (peopled by descendents of Asiatic Earth colonists), drags the mercantile democracy of Dardania into support of its corrupt government . . .

Pindaria goes to the aid of the opposition shadow government . . .

War fabers, which by now have seen action in the earliest brushfire wars, increase their numbers into the millions . . .

—Hela Fenn, Psycho-Soc
Colonial Survey, 3300 A.D.

AMONG THE MOUNTAINS

by Jack Dann

1

The men sit on their woven mats in front of the village *dinh* and pray loudly as they wait for ghostly visitations and true signs from their holy ancestors. The silvery *dinh* is the oldest structure in the village, and is now used as a longhouse and meeting place for the various clans. Just as their ancestors have done, the men shiver in the night air, gabble, pray, inhale the dark effluviums, and watch the sky.

Like a rainbow, the ring arches across a sky afire with stars and meteors.

"And I will tell you the story again," Vo Kim Lan says to the children who are playing on the mossy lawn that extends from the *dinh* to the pebble garden. The children giggle, smirk, laugh, make terrible faces, and wave their arms at him.

Because of his wrinkled face, the children call him Giay—the paper-man who can read and make up stories. He knows all the stories, and every year he makes up more. Every year he invents the world. He renames the gods and mountains and ghosts and demons and has a name for every star. He has renamed the evening star and claims that he can change the heavens with only words. He says that the mirrorlike glitterwings are holy because they are made of the same silvery stuff as the village *dinh*.

"It was on a night just like this that Tan Ming Hoang, the ruler of the world, called in his sorcerer and ordered him to construct a bridge to the stars," Giay says. He pauses, shifts his gaze from child to child. "And do you know why he wanted such a bridge?"

"I do," says a skinny twelve-year-old named Du. "Tan Ming Hoang was not happy with his world. It was not enough. He wanted Heaven too."

"That's right," says Giay. "So the sorcerer destroyed the ruler's finest palace and threw the broken pieces into the sky to make the ring you see in the sky tonight. Then he made a beautiful rainbow and told the ruler that it was the road to Heaven. The ruler left for Heaven immediately, but when he reached the sky, he found that he still couldn't touch the stars. He had been tricked."

"What then?" asks a young woman kneeling behind Du. She knows all the right questions. The ceremony is the same every year.

"When Tan Ming Hoang recognized his ruined palace, he let out a shriek and swore that he would kill the sorcerer." Giay pauses, waiting for a proper question.

"But why didn't Tan Ming Hoang kill his sorcerer?" asks Du.

"Because he could not return to the world, for the sorcerer had removed the rainbow which was the bridge to the sky. That is the reason you never see rainbows at night, only the ring. Without a rainbow, Tan Ming Hoang was stranded."

"But he could have just waited for another rainbow," Du says.

"Then he would have had to wait for daylight," says Giay. "But have you ever seen the ring in the day? It is in the sky only at night. You see, the ruler could not return."

"So what did he do?" asks Du.

"He waited, just as he waits now," Giay says. "He's still up there, looking down at us. He hates the world because he cannot have it. And he hates us. That is why he throws his stones of fire." Giay points to a meteor shower. "Yet the world doesn't burn."

All the children sigh and make *tssing* noises, as they have been instructed to do, and Giay leaves them to the women who have prepared a special feast for the solstice festival. The children will snack on *banh tet* and *dua hau,* delicious small cakes which are wrapped in mirror bush leaves and cooked over an open fire.

Giay has joined the men in prayer. They pray for the wandering souls of the dead. They pray to their ancestors and the beings who make the winds and rain. They ask for dispensation and then they recount the lives of the cross, all this to exorcise the *ma quy*—the evil souls responsible for bad crops, death, and sorrow.

It is altogether a supernatural night for both adults and children. It is a holiday of the fantastic where all thoughts and prayers and conversations are directed toward the holy ancestors and the invisible beings that crowd the air.

Bao Lam, a boy of fourteen who is now approaching his manhood, sits beside Giay and prays. He has left the place of his family to study and learn. For almost two months he has not touched the soil with his hands, has not done an errand for anyone but Giay, and—until tonight—has not even talked with his family. If he is to become a sorcerer, this will be the most important year of his life.

So he watches and listens and prays. He tries to remember the names of all the ghosts, spirits, and demons that inhabit the days and nights. Although he has learned Giay's stories and followed some of his magiks, Bao still feels like a baby and a know-nothing. But he understands that he must one day replace Giay as sorcerer, or the village will be taken by *ma quy,* all the crops will die, and his townspeople will be turned into the smoke dreams of demons and forest-ghosts.

Bao thinks it is only natural that he should become a sorcerer and follow Giay, for he was born during the equinox, on a clear night when the sky took a bite out of the ring and Charmian and Iras turned coppery red. Ever since he was old enough to understand, he has been told that his birth date was astrologically significant, for just as the ring had been broken, so would he be forced to undergo an uncertain trial.

As the men pray and wave their arms to the invisible spirits, Bao dreams of the outside world. He imagines that "everywhere" is just like the village, only inhabited by different peoples and spirits. But perhaps different magiks work in different places, he tells himself. Although he would like to venture outside the environs of his village, he is afraid, especially now that he knows Giay's prayers and stories.

He knows that if he should have the misfortune to die outside of his village, his spirit would become *ma quy.* By leaving the sacred grounds of his ancestors, he would sever all ties to the world of men. He would deny his ancestors a future—and that, he thinks, would be a terrible responsibility to bear.

But he is curious about the great war—a concept which he does not completely understand. He also wants to know more about *moi,* those boys and girls who sometimes came into the village to preach about freedom and unity, the greater family, and the holy trinity of men and soil and state. Although *moi* always spoke in Bao's language, their words were only words. He could understand the meanings of the words, but could not make sense of the general concepts.

"Wake up," says Giay, who is already standing. "Iras has lifted into the sky. Our prayers are finished for now. Stand up. Were you sleeping with the spirits?"

His vision still blurred with sleep, Bao stands up and smiles at Giay. They embrace and then walk around, nodding and shouting with the people, as they wait for the women to stoke the fires and prepare the food. Bao tries to hide his excitement under a mask of indifference, for tonight men, women, and children will remain together. The feasting and talking and praying will continue until dawn banishes Tan Ming Hoang's ring from the heavens. Tonight is a night for magiks and spirits. Bao can almost hear ghosts whispering in the wind and chattering in the fires.

"Dunk, dunk, dunk," sing the children as they wave fish-shaped lanterns to ward off noxious spirits. They dance around a *khanh,* a small gong mounted on a thirty foot pole. Clay bells and colored glass tinkle, and the village becomes the center of the world. The ring and stars and meteors are merely the gaudy lights of the village reflected in the sky.

Bao follows Giay to the edge of the pebble garden where woven mats have been laid out for them. A pregnant girl with short cropped hair brings their food: rice covered with golden flowers, sour meats, pork-plant, shed yolk, mooncakes, sugarseeds, chao gruel, bo-bread still hot and soggy, and candies that seem to bite the tongue. As tired as Bao is, he laughs and chokes down all his food. The ghosts and spirits and demons are thick in the air tonight, he thinks, and they will be watching how he performs.

After the feast the men talk, then pray, then they retire to the pebble garden to commune with their ancestors. Bao follows like a dog on a leash. He feels awkward and unsure of himself, especially now that the men look to him to help lead the prayers.

"Don't be afraid," Giay whispers to him. "You are praying to the spirits and your ancestors. Don't pay attention to the stares of old men."

After glimpsing a ghost out of the corner of his eye, Bao leads the prayers with conviction. He shouts, waves his hands just like Giay, smiles, nods to the spirits, and recites all the prayers and proper singsongs. The night goes quickly. By the time Charmian is in the sky, the children are asleep with aunts, sisters, mothers, and grandmothers. They are all safely inside the *dinh* where washing bowls and morning wine have been set out on mats for the men.

The men are still praying and talking, although some of the oldest are nodding. But tonight the men must remain conscious to ward off the spirits and *ma quy* that would enter their mouths to take their souls. Bao fights sleep by staring at a *bat quai,* an intricate design painted on a piece of turned wood. His studies with Giay have been rigorous; there has been little time for sleep. As he plays with the wood, turning it over and over in his hand, he wonders when Giay ever finds time to sleep. Giay is an old man, Bao tells himself. Yet buried inside that old husk is a playful little boy. Bao looks into the concentric lines of the *bat quai*. He draws himself into the design. Imagines that his old age is buried inside him. And with his eyes wide open, he dreams of dragons and numbers . . .

The blaring of horns wakes the village.

Although the rest of the men entered the *dinh* at dawn, Bao and Giay are still outside singing the last prayers for ancestors and village spirits. It is early morning and Caesar is driving the purple shadows from the mountains. A few clouds scud overhead, as if trying to escape from the sun.

"*Moi* have returned," Bao says to Giay, but the old man's face retains its fixed expression. Bao watches as the noisy parade makes its way through the village. First come the boys and girls dressed in costumes of black and red. They wave flags and swing incense tapers back and forth. They are followed by other *moi* dressed in festival costume: a black dragon with green paper teeth and orange claws, a great fish with faces peeping out of its gill-slits, silvery sectos hung on the branches of walking trees, a king gator which cannot quite co-ordinate its movements, a hoplite wearing slippers, a hipposaur, and a big polypus with red paper tentacles. Then come young men and women who shout and smile and drop papers which bear the *bat quai* symbol. And then come the trumpeteers who are followed by fabers. The fabers dance and mimic the *moi*. With their short arms and strangely jointed legs, their iridescent scales reflecting the morning sun, and their great golden eyes, they look like human grotesques.

Bao imagines that the fabers are inhabited by demons, and he remembers what Giay had once told him: "Every man—and animal, too—might be driven by ghosts and demons. A demon can enter your mouth as you breathe. Once inside you, it will take your thoughts and force you to live in its dreams. So you must be careful, lest you yawn and find that *ma quy* has stolen your thoughts."

"Why do *moi* parade for us?" Bao asks Giay who is tweaking his thin gauzy whiskers.

"The outsiders come to teach us their ways," Giay says, picking up a piece of the *moi's* yellow paper which a breeze has carried along the ground. "They think they can show us a new world by dancing about and dropping *bat quay* and singing the variations of the alphabet. But they think that *their* world is the real one. They think only *their* world produces correct dreams. Have you talked with *moi*?"

Bao nods his head.

"Then you know that they have different dreams. We have no such need for dreams to guide our every action—the demons could do that well enough, if we let them. Their words and dreams are without meaning, just as they are empty. They are phantoms, shadows that can speak and withstand light."

"Then what do they want with us?" Bao asks.

"They think they can change us and pull us into their dreams, Giay says. "But we will not take new things—new magiks—or we tear away our roots. And our roots are in this ground, not in the neverlands or shadows of the caves. Those other worlds cannot have meaning for us and, if you are to become a sorcerer, you must learn to make *moi* disappear. You must see through them, as if they were demons or *ma quy*."

"But I can see them," Bao says, watching a young woman dance about. She looks at Bao and smiles, then skips away.

"What do you see?" Giay asks.

"Just what you see. *Moi*."

"And you know that *moi* are only shadows. What do you hear?"

"I hear songs and shouts and horns and the clanging of bells," Bao says.

"Tell me again what you really see," Giay says as he closes his eyes, and Bao remembers what he has been told about the snakes of time and all the difficult paths to sight. So Bao counts and dreams of dragons and tries to find his own snake of time. He travels in circles, as if following the lines of a *bat quay*. Then he is outside of his seconds and minutes—he has found his snake and is peering into its dreams. The snake dreams of Bao. And time crawls along very slowly.

"Now open your eyes," Giay says. "What do you see?"

Bao laughs and says, "I see shadows."

"And what do you hear?"

"I hear the tinkling of bellflowers and the buzzbuzz and tssings of sectos," Bao says as he watches his neighbors leave the safety of the *dinh* and join the parade. Old men and women dance about, as if to the beating rhythms of their strong hearts. Children rush into the melee. They laugh and wave their arms. Although Bao can no longer see *moi,* he senses them as a directing force, a force which will quickly pass through the village and into some impossible world of dreams. Meanwhile, Bao sits and watches and smiles and yawns noisily for his ancestors who might seek passage into his soul.

"Now you can see clearly," Giay says. "What you see with your eyes is not always real. Your mind can see much more clearly." Then Giay stands and walks briskly toward the crowd of dancers. Villagers move out of his way, for he walks like Duc, the blind beggar who brings luck to any farmer who feeds him. Giay turns, both arms outstretched, and shouts for Bao to follow.

Reluctantly, Bao joins his teacher and prays that his eyes will not fail him by admitting false visions and shadows. "Why do we do this?" Bao asks Giay as they weave through the crowd. Bao tries to ignore the phantoms that dance beside him and disappear when he turns to look directly at them. He prays to exorcise the unseen monsters that jabjabb and chitter and sound like stormwinds soughing through windertrees.

"We do this to show our kinsmen that shadows are

not people, that they must be ignored, that they do not exist except as false visions inside our heads."

"But no one will pay attention," Bao says. "They will see what they see."

"No," says Giay. "They will see what they want to see, what they must see. Our burden is to lead them in the proper direction."

"And how do you know that direction?"

Giay looks upward, as if to share a joke with heaven, and laughs. "Why, all the ghosts and spirits are shouting the correct answers. Every ancestor of every ancestor points out the same direction. Just listen to them. Look at them."

Bao looks around, and sees that some of the children are already miming Giay. They walk around as if they are blind. Their arms are extended before them. Nut-brown faces smile, as if the very young could reflect the very old. Bao can almost believe that Giay has taken them over, that he is hiding behind their dark eyes and baby faces. Then the adults, taking their cues from the children, become blind to *moi*. Soon Giay and Bao are the center of the group. Once again the village is its own world, governed by its own laws and spirits.

"So you see," Giay says, "the *moi* are easily defeated by the ghosts of our land. The village is as it was."

Giay and Bao lead the villagers away from the shadows of *moi*. The sun has climbed higher into the sky. Bao looks upward and gives thanks to the spirits that cluster about him, even though they are invisible. But he looks away from the sun, for Caesar is the blinding eye of God.

The holiday is over. Magic must give way to work. It is time to return to hutches and fields and paddies. Bao looks past a row of hutches and imagines that even now women wearing loose trousers, conical hats made of silverleaf, and wooden clogs, are working in the rice paddies beside the dynobryon forest which climbs up the steep face of a mountainside. But somewhere in the mountains is the door-through-the-world. Giay claims it is a huge cave built by giants. He says that anyone who steps into the darkness of the cave will find himself back on Earth, the hell which burns forever in cold flames.

Suddenly the sky darkens. Storm clouds appear like phantoms skating on blue ice. Thunder rolls in the distance. And the villagers run for cover. Bao looks around, sees only the familiar faces of village folk and the *moi*-shadows. Time seems to slow down as the world awaits a deluge. It is *mua mura,* the rainy season, a special time to reaffirm the sacred ties of family, neighbor, and clan.

Then, an instant later, the world collapses. The village is attacked. Villagers fall to the ground as if play-acting. Drops of rain fall like tiny bombs. Mist seems to be pouring out of the ground. Every sound is magnified, as if in a dream, but there are only sharp screams and the crackcrack of rifles.

Another instant and the village is afire. Hutches are burning, their woven bamboo walls and sarissa roofs swelling into flame, burning with a popping and cackling, as if ghosts and demons are laughing and mashing their teeth. Soldiers and fabers dressed in filthy green and brown uniforms run across the mud, then disappear in the mist. But the fires they set glow redly in the storm created twilight.

Bao shakes his head, as if a dream could be broken or thrown aside by a simple gesture. Demons are running around, burning, shooting, raping girls and women in the open, in the mud and rain. But *moi* are also falling. *Moi* are killing *moi,* Bao thinks. They are only men, Bao tells himself, surprised that he is lying on the ground under cover of rotbush and crying vines. He tastes the bitter soil and wonders if he is hurt or dying.

He watches the pregnant girl who had brought him his dinner being raped. Help her, he tells himself, but he is frozen. He cannot move a finger, and he has wet his pants. He cries, then breaks out of his fright, stands up, and rushes toward the *moi* and the shrieking girl. The girl stops screaming. Perhaps she's dead, Bao thinks. He feels he is trapped in a dream of slow motion.

He wrests the rifle from the *moi* and shoots the demon in the head. But it isn't a demon, he tells himself. It isn't even a man, just a boy with a shaved head. The girl beneath the dead *moi* does not move, does not even seem to notice Bao. Her hair is full of mud, and her face is bleeding. Bao sees that her nose is broken.

Get out of here, he thinks as a fusillade of shots breaks the momentary calm. The air smells sour. The downpour is over. A light drizzle falls from an angry grey sky. Soon the mist will lift. Bao shivers and sees that his rain-soaked overshirt is spattered with *moi* blood.

He stands up, looking for Giay, forgetting for an instant about the attack. But Giay is nowhere to be seen. Perhaps he's dead and demons have carried his body into the sky, Bao thinks. He dreams, then remembers where he is, and runs. He runs across the pebble garden and past burning hutches and trees, past the well-kept shrubs and Venus Mirrors which smell sweet and heavy. Dead bodies litter the ground. Bao hears commands barked in a familiar tongue. *Don day. Durng lai. Tuan lenh khong toi ban.* But the tones and accents are wrong. The words are slurred, as if spoken by drunken men.

But Bao does not think about orders or bodies or burning hutches. He has forgotten Giay, the pregnant girl, the dead *moi,* the smells of death and feces and urine, the fusillades of shots, the rain, the mist, the screams. He thinks only of his family. Perhaps they are alive. His family had left the solstice celebration early. They did not even eat with their neighbors, for Giay had told them that Bao would lead the last prayers. From now on, Giay had said, Bao could have no family but the village.

The sky begins to clear. The mist lifts, disappears as if it had never been.

Bao runs blindly, and the universe lets him pass. He feels he has already lost his soul to some *ma quy* which is too powerful to be exorcised. He imagines that he is a shadow, no better than *moi*. Perhaps that is why *moi* can't see me, he thinks. But he tells himself that he is being prepared for something else. Just as the ring was eaten by the sky when he was born, so must the path of his life be dark and difficult. But why must my path to the cross lead me home? he asks the imagined spirits of the air.

He skirts the rice fields and smells the swamp-stink of stagnant water. He imagines that he has become two beings. One being watches the other. It talks, tells the other being that time is still passing. The other being listens and screams.

Bao sees his house, a medium-sized hutch built of sarissa, wood, and mud. It overlooks a canal which irrigates the adjacent rice paddy.

He runs across open land dotted with sarissa and Christmas memory. It has become a beautiful morning. The sun has burned away the clouds, the sky is a cool blue, and the sectos are buzzing as if to prevent the world from going dumb. Bao is trapped in a pastel dream where spirits rule kindly and the sun always shines.

But when he enters his hutch, he finds his mother and father and sister hanging upside down from a ceiling truss. His mother and sister are naked. They are all bound with brown rope. And they are all, clearly, dead. Light beams cut into the darkness like yellow swords.

He sits down on a woven mat before the hearth. Cooking utensils have been strewn over the hard-packed dirt floor. Bowls are broken, bark baskets torn apart. The cramped family room is heavy with body stink and the sweet smells of gravy-oil, moon cakes, sugar-seed breads, bamba peels, glazed meat, shed yolk, roasted carryseeds, wine, and milk-liquor. Four places have been set before the hearth, each with wiping cloth, eating sticks, and a painted bowl. One of the settings is for the wandering spirit who brings good luck, long life, and happiness. Bao tries not to look at the wood-plank bed on the other side of the hearth. The reed pad is soiled with blood. But the altar is in its proper place against the wall. It seems that *moi* did not wish to antagonize the spirits of the hut.

Taking the food sticks in his hand, Bao makes a blessing over the food and begins to eat. With every mouthful of festival food, he feels more removed from the apparent world of cause and effect. And he descends, as if through the scrim-layers of a gentle dream, to a synchronistic universe. He drifts backwards, only to be swallowed by the snake of time. Now he finds everything is just as it should be. He is in perfect harmony with *ying* and *yang,* the two opposing forces of the universe. He is easily transformed. He dreams that the universe is a wheel. Every event must repeat itself in slightly different form. Flesh and spirit are themselves movements of the great wheel.

He watches as all the cycles reveal themselves. He feels possessed by Heaven's will. I must remain here in this house, he tells himself. Then he prays to the spirits of the dead and the not-yet-here, to the monsters and ghosts of the past, and the growing spirit-creatures of the future. Bao sees only with his mind. He falls into his past, dreams that he is eating and talking with his family. He has captured all the familiar smells and words, all the textures of time past. If I can feel the past as the present, then I have turned the wheel, he tells himself. I have truly left this cycle and journeyed to a gentler time.

But his eyes betray him. He finds himself staring at the dead bodies of his mother and father and sister. They have become empty husks; their spirits have escaped from their open mouths. Bao has not been watchful. He has lost their souls. They have drifted away to become *ma quy*.

With a scream, he stands up and pummels his father's corpse with his fists. He screams for death, for its bone-crushing touch, and hopes that *moi* will hear him and end his life right now. A timely death would be the perfect resolution. Perhaps he can still join the spirits of his family.

Bao sits down in front of his father, then retreats into gentle dreams. He looks at his father's upside-down face and imagines that the hutch is filled with sympathetic spirits. They make the air heavy. They smell of grass and sweat and night effluviums. They have the faces of his family.

"Remain here," says his dead father without moving his lips. Bao ignores the spirit-voice inside his head. It might be a demon or false spirit trying to trick him.

"You must listen to your father," says his dead mother. *"Your path must end here. You must remain with us, for only through you can we have any spirit-life. You close the circle of our existence. Together, we are like the great wheel. We belong to you now. And you belong to this house, to the soil and the wood and sarissa, and to every ghost in the air."*

Bao understands that death must not be an end, but a transition. He remembers Giay's words: "Man is a breeze, stilled only by death. Then he becomes like the earth. But the earth is sacred and must be maintained by prayer. Each generation must sing the same prayers or our ancestors will be cut off from the world."

"You cannot leave," says Bao's father. *"Your past and future lie here."*

"You must provide for your ancestors," says his dead sister. *"When we are buried in sacred soil, we will not be able to follow you. You must not leave."*

"You must provide," sing the spirits.

"No," Bao says to the dead. He steps out of the hutch and shouts, "Where are you, *moi?* I am here.

Kill me." The world whispers, but will not listen. Wind soughs through sarissa and highvine. Sectos chirp and buzz. A hipposaur lows in the distance.

Bao walks away from the hutch and the paddies and the village. He does not look for cover. If *moi* cannot kill him, then he will find the door-through-the-world. He will enter the cave built by giants and descend into hell.

He skirts the edge of Ban Dem Forest where spruce, pine, willow, and oak create a twilight world for sleeping demons and shadowy ghosts. It is as if the tall trees are waging a slow battle for space and light with the indigenous yellow-crawlers, flatfronds, and the weblike silverfrost. Bao's feet pad upon a soft tuff which is a spongy mulch of dead leaves, crawlers, and rot. He cries, hacking out his pain and loss as if they are pieces of raw meat. The forest absorbs his noises. He retreats into the dark world of bough and leaf. The spirits of family and village cannot follow him here. They are lost to him forever. By simple intention, Bao has become *moi*. He has decided to die outside of the village. He has broken the circle and smashed the wheel. And like the circle, Bao is broken. One half of him is rage, the other half is quiet: *ying* and *yang*. The circle is true, even when broken.

Dark forest gives way to scrub and mossy uplands. Bao detours around silvernets which have trapped small winebirds and silver flyers. Forest green has been replaced by the umbers and ochers of high ground. Swarms of smidgins darken the air like storm clouds. They fly toward Bac Mountain, to the door-through-the-world where all manner of beasts and Hell's monsters are spawned.

It is early afternoon when Bao reaches the crags and sheer rock faces of Bac Mountain. He begins his climb to the roof of the world. He has defected from the world of men. Here, among the mountains, he is less than a demon, more fragile than a ghost. He has lost past and future. All that is left to him is the constant present. But his soul cannot be confined in such a narrow place. As Giay had said, "The soul is a flower made of the very stuff of time. Its soil is the past, its air is the present, its water is the future. If we forget our past, or are blind to our future, then the soul wilts and dies. We become husks without hearts."

Bao climbs until he is exhausted. He has worked his way from ledge to ledge, foothold to foothold. The sun hangs in the clear sky like an angry eye. It watches Bao and saps his strength. There is no shade, no cover for a *moi* climbing into Hell. The world has turned to stone. Below him, the blue-black shadows are as tangible as the blades of butcher knives. Above him is the door-through-the-world.

It takes him an hour to reach the stone lip of the cave. He crawls through a narrow passageway into darkness. Now he can die. The shadow-spirits can take him. He shivers, feels cold stone against his cheek. Gradually, his eyes adjust to the darkness and he sees stalagmite towers in the distance. The cave is aglow with a cold phosphorescent light. Bao imagines that he has come upon a subterranean city. The rainbow-hued stalagmites and stalactites might be the grotesque dwellings of the dead. He might be bathing in the cold light of Hell.

"I am here," he shouts, and his voice, carried by ghosts and demons, echoes through the subterranean halls. But the dead will not answer him. They mock him with his own words. He walks on, through the many chambers of the dead. He is soon lost in the caverns, some of which are completely dark.

He loses his sense of time. He sleeps and walks and dreams. His hunger is a constant, a dull ache which he imagines to be his companion. He dreams of his father. He dreams of *moi,* the weapons of God. The caverns are full of scrabbling, chittering life. It is a dark universe of worms and clickers and scuttlers.

Reptiles splash in unseen pools and bats shriek for lost spirits. White-winged moths fly overhead like ghosts floating in darkness.

Bao dreams of bright light. He crawls out of the darkness, as if he is stepping out of time. He has smashed the wheel of his life. He falls and vomits. Demons rush out of his mouth.

In his dream, the creatures stand above him and talk. He cannot understand their words. He wonders how long he has been in the caverns. He dreams of his village and begins to shake.

But it is too late, Bao thinks. He is dead, just another *moi.* He dreams that his spirit has already become *ma quy,* a demon wanderer. He touches the edges of his dream and pushes toward the darkness that is either death or empty sleep. . . .

2

Lying in a prone position, Bao Lam peered through a field glass at the valley below. It was as he remembered it, only more verdant and beautiful. The forests were in bloom, their colors so bright that they confused all sense of distance and space. Foreground and background seemed to bleed into each other. As he used to do in his childhood, he counted all the colors of choehoa—the pastel-tinted pseudoblooms. In his old language, the equivalent word for color was light-of-god.

Below him, past the straw-colored rock, below the small brown fists of scrub, the land became a green mat of moss sloping gently downward to meet a forest of saucerleaves. Shiny green and yellow fronds swayed in the wind. Vines of silverglitter reflected the twelve o'clock sun, and Bao could make out a copse of redknob. He turned up the magnification to see if the sweet-smelling plants had attracted any flyers. Seeing that the sticky knobs were covered with rotting carcasses, he quickly looked away. He remembered the stink, the furrowed surface, the sticky ooze of redknob. He remembered the burning sores it had once left on his fingers.

He searched the entire valley with his field glass, carefully scanning an area from right to left, raising the glass and scanning again. When he caught sight of a rice field, he stepped up the magnification and watched several women transplanting rice seedlings. The water reflected the bright colors of the world. Bao imagined that these women were dipping their hands into rainbows.

Although Mun Village was well hidden, Bao knew its exact location. He felt as if he could see through the barriers of flora, past saucerleaves and silverglitter, past oak and yellow-crawlers and scatter bush and high sarissa, right into the sleepy little village which was its own world. This was the heart of Casca Mountain country. Bao knew that this hidden village would look like every other village he had passed through. It was as if he had spent his childhood and the long years of the war in the same village. It was a *ching*-game. He followed his programmed dreams, led dimsimple fabers, watched them die, won villages, lost villages, hid, slept, and fought. He had lost the past and future. He was a blind spirit submerged in a dead present. He had dreams and food and fabers. He was a child of the people.

"Take your group around the ricefield and enter the village from the north," Bao said to Le, one of his two command fabers. Le's face had a different structure than the simple soldier: a high forehead and small crest, a flexible mouth that could form words and express basic emotion. "Call in, and I'll follow with Chi."

Chi, who was a double for Le, remained beside Bao as Le rose and screeched at the company of fabers. The soldiers had grouped behind Bao. They kneeled, as if praying, their large yellow eyes looking blankly upon a world they were not engineered to comprehend.

"So now we wait," Bao said, ostensibly to Chi, but he was only talking to himself. He watched the women in the field through his field glass and tried to ignore Chi and the remaining fabers. As he stared at the women, looking for something unusual, any change in their rooster-walk movement, he felt all the walls of the world separating him from his own kind. These villagers seemed more alien to him than his green stick-figure soldiers. Perhaps, he thought, if I look into a mirror, I would find that I have become a faber. He turned to Chi, who sat beside him and stared ahead, as if into nothingness. The faber's scaly armor was iridescent in the sunlight.

Bao turned his field glass toward the women again and tried to imagine the people of this village. There was time for a *ching*-game. He dreamed of *Pi,* the image of grace, and he shaped his dream as if he was making love to one of the slender girls working in the paddy. But *Pi* is composed of *Ken,* the mountain, and *Le,* the fire. *Fire at the foot of the mountain: the image of grace.* The dream grew dark as Bao manipulated *Po,* the inferior forces, and the dream-world of the girls in the paddy shattered like glass.

"Village clear," said Le's voice amidst radio static.

"Take your group and clean out every hutch," Bao said to Chi. Bao did not expect trouble. The mountain people had become passive to the comings and goings of their war of liberation. They had taught themselves not to 'see' the enemy. And the few who could be trained to fight changed sides as often as they ate. The war was like a *ching*-game, Bao thought, but it was a game directed by unseen forces, forces Bao could only imagine.

Bao waited and watched the girls working in the field. He wondered what it would be like to have a woman, then shuddered, remembering his mother and sister hanging like carcasses on redknob. But his memory of mother and sister was quickly pushed out of his mind. Almost as quickly as the thought had surfaced, it was forgotten. Bao had no need of such memories; he had *ching*-games to replace the pains of the past. He had the present.

He heard shots, short bursts echoing, as if carried from the village by gleeful demons.

"Ambush." Chi's voice was raspy over the radio.

"Where are they?" Bao asked, speaking into a tiny ovoid communicator. He held the communicator close to his lips, as if *moi* could hear him, as if they were standing right behind him, listening, but afraid to kill him. That would ruin the game.

The static was a barrage of tiny explosions, the quickened sounds of guns and shouting and death. "They have moved back to the silverglitter. I have ten soldiers left. Moving them out."

Bao heard more shots, but he was already moving, directing his remaining fabers. He remained several paces behind the group for safety, but four fabers guarded him, protected him with their scaly bodies, mimed his every action like green shadows born out of a dream. But Bao paid them no attention. They were merely a part of his surroundings. They might as well have been walking plants or stones. They lived and died without awareness like simple beasts. They had no past or future, only a present.

The shots had become sporadic. Bao imagined that *moi* had once again left the silverglitter and were carefully cleaning out one hutch after another. Perhaps the *moi* attack was a fluke, he thought. Or more likely, they had known his whereabouts. *Moi* might be behind him right now, tracking him like silent animals patient for their kill. And Bao knew that nearby a Pindarian missionary was directing his attack. If only I could get *him,* Bao thought.

Bao would not reply to Chi. Perhaps he could still gain some surprise. Walking through the saucerleaf forest that flanked the western edge of the village, he felt that only an instant had passed since he was a child running from his village, from *moi* and demons and family spirits. An instant ago his life was before him—to learn, conjure, marry, bear children, pray for his ancestors and the world. But he had broken the cycle and was now condemned to an eternal empty present. He thought about the war and this place, and concluded that he understood nothing. He was under the control of demons who wore pink faces and had given him tools and *ching*-dreams. He had all the correct memories and information. He knew every mile of this country, even the places he had never seen.

As if waking from a recurring dream, he forgot, once again, what it was all about. He could only remember *ching*-games. Everything around him seemed to be in constant motion. The fronds made sushing sounds as he slid past them. The supple saucerleaves were slippery to the touch and veined as if they were great pieces of green flesh. The faber-soldiers moved smoothly through their natural habitat, as if they had never been biologically engineered to be fodder for a war of liberation. The ground was spongy. It was a floral cemetery of dead leaves, humus, twigs, crawlers. Colorful pseudoblooms flourished everywhere, giving a colorful palette to what would otherwise be a monotonous green and yellow world. Bao had a sudden desire to take off his boots and run through the forest in his bare feet.

Bao had thought to surprise the *moi* in the brush, but he could find no sign of *moi*. Everything was quiet. Too quiet, Bao thought. He directed his fabers to enter the village just north of the *dinh*. They leapfrogged from hutch to hutch, keeping away from the pebble garden and mossy open ground. Dead fabers and villagers littered the village common area, the place of *thinh hoang,* the village guardian spirit. They looked like wooden figures, spirit-dolls dropped by hungry children called to dinner.

Bao remained behind, using a ramshackle deserted hutch for cover. There were several hutches on the edge of the village which were maintained for lesser spirits. Bao felt the forest's presence, as if it was an enemy staring at the back of his neck. He did not move. He sensed something was about to happen. It was a soldier's sense, a smell, a tickle which became a pressure between his eyes, centered in his pineal.

He recognized Le, who was lying dead in the pebble garden, his arms and part of his chest blown away by a *moi* projectile. Bao began to scan the village with his field glass. And the enemy opened fire on him. He hit the ground. The hutch was in flames. It began to fall, spreading out on the ground, sending out feelers of fire. Bao's fabers returned the fire, and a few *moi* fell. But they were moving toward Bao. He was worth a thousand fabers.

You were sloppy, he told himself as the ground exploded. Yet he felt he had enough time to think and dream. Everything was moving in slow motion. Soon the world would freeze. But right now demons were walking about, tearing the guts out of his town.

His town. That was how he had thought of it. He felt as if he was back in his village. Why not die here? he thought.

"Because we won't have you." A ghost whispered inside his head. It was the memory of his childhood. It was Giay. It was his parents. His ancestors. All dead. All living in the air, wandering because of him. Die, he thought, but just the same, he crawled back into the forest like a scuttler seeking darkness. His shoulder felt cold and numb; it was oozing blood. Bao wondered just where the bullet had lodged—if it was a bullet. It

might have passed right through him. Don't look, he told himself. It doesn't matter. It doesn't hurt yet. You'll go into shock. In shock now. He thought of Giay, imagined that the ghost was crawling before him, motioning him forward.

"You remember how to 'see,'" Giay said. *"You must will* moi *out of existence. Push them from your thoughts. Think of the village. That is where your ancestors and friends and family live. The rest is emptiness. Ignore* moi-*demons."*

Bao crawled in the forest, his hands digging into damp black dirt, his eyes staring ahead at a ghost. He felt the earth's coolness and the weight of a green and yellow world above him. It was as if he was at the bottom of an ocean. He was a water-spirit about to fall asleep as he looked up at the seafronds and weeds swaying gently to the silent music of cool blue water.

You are sloppy, he told himself. And this isn't even your village. The past can't kill me, he thought. My ancestors are *ma quy*. Dead spirits. They'd have no use for a *moi*-soldier.

He remembered his slogans and *ching*-games. He remembered his 'life-dreams' which had usurped his past. Slogans and *ching*-variations ran in his mind like wheels of words and memories. The wheels turned, sparking familiar slogans.

"You are a child of the people," shrieked the voices inside his head. They drawled out old lessons, reminded him of obligations. And Bao realized that he had never seen a city, although he had dreamed that he was once inside one. He had never taken a fly-by, dressed-up, hooked-in, read a book, watched a holo, or loved a woman. Memories roiled like smoke from burning hutches. He began to dream, creating a *ching*-game, but he forced himself awake. He reached for memories. He had memories, he told himself. They must count for something. But were his memories real? Perhaps only *ching*-games and life-dreams were real.

I have seen things, he said to himself. But he could not quite remember what he had seen. He felt as if he had always been in these forests. His life was this land. He had always skulked through villages, fought *moi,* eaten rations, directed fabers, talked to villagers who would not believe his slogans because he was a soldier. He belonged to the land, yet he had lost his village and his ancestors.

When had he last talked to a human being? He could not remember. Yes, he thought. I have talked to— He remembered that he had talked to his fabers.

"You have become a faber," Giay said. He sat in lotus position under a huge dynobryon.

"I'll return to our village," Bao said to the ghost. "I'll pray for my ancestors and become a sorcerer."

"You have no village," Giay said. *Everyone you know is dead."*

And as Bao fell toward dreamless sleep, he heard Giay say: *"You are already dead."*

"You must not remain here," Chi said, pulling Bao to his feet. Bao's shoulder was bandaged and felt sticky. His chest ached. He felt numbed and tired. He imagined that he was caught in hookervine. He could not move or think. But he was a soldier. And the slogans were still wheeling.

"Report," Bao said. Once again, he felt as if he had two selves. He was two beings, each one fighting for control. His darker, more subterranean self, howled gleefully.

"You are approximately fifteen miles west of the village. You have thirty-two soldiers. Le is dead. Wounded were left behind. The soldiers are in spread retreat. I carried you under cover."

Bao looked around, but could not see any soldiers, though he was sure they were nearby. They would be well hidden and without uniform. If *moi* happened upon them, the soldiers would be mistaken for natural fabers.

As Chi carried him through dense forest, Bao slept fitfully. He dreamed he was crawling through a dark cave. He dreamed that he could crawl backwards into his previous life. "Am I dead?" he mumbled, dreaming of Giay's ghost. He could not remember. Do I have family? he asked himself. Or am I a soldier? Always fighting. Never praying. A child of the state. No, he thought, as if he was caught midway between darkness and light. He dreamed of imaginary places. I do other things, he told himself. I know other things.

"What do I know?" Bao asked Chi. He grabbed the faber's scaly arm which held him gently. It was cool to the touch.

When Bao awakened, it was dark and humid. The air was still, Charmian was in the sky, and stars shown through the dimly glowing dust of the ring. Bao could make out Orion and the constellations of *the buckle, the two fishermen, the smidgens, the khanh, the serpent,* and *the ship*. He knew the sky; it contained all the shapes of his dreams. It was a silent friend, this resting place of spirits and ancestors.

Shifting his gaze from the bright night sky, he looked past the cliffs and canyons of Casca country to the Northern Mountains in the distance. As a child, Bao had been told that friendly spirits had pulled the mountains out of the ground to keep out *moi* and demons. But demons passed through the mountains and took their revenge.

Bao traced his fingers along his shoulder wound. There was still some pain, but he could move about. Nothing had broken. Chi had worried out the bullet and applied fastflesh to quicken the healing process. Bao counted himself lucky that the bullet had not been treated with a sacworm poison or scored so it would explode on impact.

As Bao stared at Chi, he was reminded of a machine that had been shut off until it would be needed again. Chi stood perfectly still, as if he was a great scaly plant which grew among saucerleaf and yellow-crawlers. Bao understood that the altered fabers were sauroids, and were related to hipposaurs, gators, hoplites, and the huge-winged flying deltasaurs.

"Try control post again, and we'll get moving," Bao said to Chi. Bao was worried. He had not been able to contact control post or base *hai,* which was his assigned recovery area. As he had very few soldiers, he could at least make a reconnaisance of base *hai* and try to discover what was wrong.

Bao looked away as the faber raised the ovoid radio transceiver and began to speak. If Bao did not look at Chi, he could pretend that the faber was human. He needed the illusion that he was not alone. But the faber could not carry on an extended conversation. It could respond to questions and follow orders, and—under certain circumstances—could even initiate action. But the faber had no soul, Bao thought. It was a biological machine with a life only for the state.

If only I had a laser transceiver, Bao thought. But it was enough that he had rations and fabers and weapons. Movement was the key to a guerrilla war. It was the engine of revolution. Each man commanded his own army. He was given an order and an objective. Then he was on his own.

Bao stood up and motioned to Chi to start moving. Chi, in turn, motioned to the soldiers. Although Bao could not see the other fabers, he knew their approximate positions. They were spread out in a wide fan formation. If they were discovered by *moi,* the soldiers would draw the enemy fire while Bao took cover.

As Bao walked through rough country, he listened intently to the nightsounds—the scratchings and clickings of sectos, the shushings of breezes through flatvine and saucerleaves, the faraway crashings of white water.

A bluebat shrieked and, as if in reply, a mountain-hog howled. Bao imagined that he was working his way through another life-dream, one that he had not experienced before. The world was trying to speak to him. It was full of dream-figures. He only had to recognize them. He looked to the north and imagined that the chalky cliffs which formed a long uneven palisade were demon's teeth. Beyond the cliffs were mountains shrouded in mist.

Bao kept to rocky terrain which afforded sufficient cover from *moi* and avoided the fieldmoss of open ground. When he reached Nho Forest, he took a last look at the cliffs. He remembered that the meaning of any life-dream depended on the interaction of *ying* and *yang*. And he comprehended his fears. The world had become an enemy that concealed all manner of ghosts and demons. He was afraid of the very ground that protected him from *moi*.

He did not stop to rest until he was out of the forest. Before him was hill country where he would find mossland, fields, paddies, villages, and, farther west, base *hai*. The cold grey light of dawn had turned the world into a misty ghostland. Bao waited, and shivered in the dampness. His chest and shoulder still hurt, the pain pulsing as if to keep time with his heartbeat. He could not just take a pill and move on. He would have to sleep. He needed to dream, experience a familiar life-dream, or play the *ching*-game. But he could not find a dream. He was wide-awake.

The soldiers sounded the alarm. It was the high whine of the wild faber.

Bao stayed behind as Chi reconnoitered, then followed when the faber waved that it was safe. Chi led him to a mossy rill flanked on all sides by earth elm and Christmas memory which were fighting an impossibly slow war for space and light. About twenty Dardanian fabers lay dead, as if sleeping on the cool moss under the shade of the trees. They were all wearing the same colors as Bao, except some of the uniforms had been torn open.

Bao was met by their stink, which was almost human —it was the universal smell of death, of rotting flesh and trapped feces. But as Bao examined them, he began to panic, as if this was the first time he had encountered death. Once again, he felt as if he was dreaming. He remembered entering a hutch and finding his mother and father and sister hanging upside down from a ceiling truss. He remembered running across open land dotted with sarissa and Christmas memory. He dreamed that he was going home again.

The soldiers had died of the plague, the great weapon which would end the war and turn all the people into children of the land. Bao had listened to the propaganda. As he understood it, the faber-specific plague would destroy only *moi*-fabers. All Dardanian fabers were to be immunized.

Then why weren't these fabers immunized? Bao asked himself as he stared at them. Their scale-plates had begun to fall away from their flesh which had turned color. The fabers were bloated. He found oozing sores under their loose scales.

The plague was not supposed to do this, Bao thought. It was just supposed to kill like smoke poison or a bullet to the heart. He felt himself begin to dream. He could dream, yet remain awake. He had been taught to dream by the state. Just as dreams were supposed to replace dead memories, so would the revolution erase the past.

In the dew-dampness of morning, the world was a new and colorful place. The sun, which had burned its way into a clear sky, was now blurred by clouds skiffing past. Great cumulus clouds soon closed up the sky as they moved like great silent engines made of air. Then lightning shot like chords of gold from cloud to cloud, followed by the crack and crash of thunder. The earth boomed, as if the sky was a tight skin which demons were pounding and trying to tear. And there was a deluge. A mist rose in response.

Bao walked stoically through the rain. He ignored the ache in his chest and shoulder. The wound was healing. When he reached base *hai,* he could rest and sleep while Chi reconnoitered. But now he would use the rain for cover. *Moi* would have difficulty finding him in this downpour.

The storm raged for another hour, then suddenly ended, leaving a mist on the land. Beyond the next rise was a base *hai,* the small farming village that had been taken so easily from *moi* last year. When the Dardanians had directed their forces to the north, the *moi* retreated into the South. So base *hai,* formerly Son La, was now inside the triangle of Dardanian-held country. But the lines constantly shifted. And another *moi* offensive was due.

When Bao stopped to rest, the mist had lifted. The clouds had scudded away like frightened white animals. The world was bright and clean. Bao felt the warmth of sun on his face as he gazed at the valley below. A mossy lawn of varying shades of green gave way to furrowed fields and paddies. An irrigation canal reflected the morning sun into a stream of molten gold. Even without a field glass, Bao could make out the village hutches and part of the *dinh.* But something was wrong. There were no women in the fields, which was unusual, as this was prime working time. The rootstalks had to be tended daily. They resembled high sarissa, but were extremely light sensitive. By nightfall they would be submerged in the muddy water of the paddy. Like waterweed, rootstalks glowed under water.

Bao sent Chi and a few soldiers to scout around the village. In the meantime, he scanned the village and its environs with his field glass. He could not see anyone about. No smoke rose from any of the hutches he could see. He scanned the paddies and fields, even the forest and scrubland. He had time for a *ching*-game. It would renew him, give him peace of mind and proper thoughts. But he had become uncomfortable with his dreams lately. Just as *yin* was not wholly *yin*, so the medicine could become a poison. When Bao dreamed, forgotten memories rose out of his unconscious like prehistoric creatures crawling out of the darkness.

Once again, Bao tried to dream, play a *ching*-game. He dreamed of *Tun*. But *Tun* is composed of *Ch'ien*, the heavens, and *Ken* the mountain. *Mountain under heaven: the image of retreat*. The dream grew dark, and Bao saw himself as a child beating his dead father. The *ching*-game was spoiled.

He felt nauseated and feverish when he came out of the dream. The fastflesh should have taken care of any infection, he told himself as he bent over, touching his knees with his chin. No more dreams, he thought. Such memories could not serve the state.

It was early afternoon before Chi called in. So far, the fabers had found nothing. Bao told Chi to search the village and report what he found. Although his shoulder still hurt, Bao felt rested after a heavy dream-ridden sleep. He felt warm, but not feverish. The nausea had not returned.

"The village has been checked," Chi said. His voice sounded raspy over the transceiver. "All the hutches are clear of villagers. Many villagers are dead."

"What have they died from?" Bao asked, looking at the familiar cliffs and gutted hills which spread to the north. Perhaps *moi* had swept through on a raid, he thought.

"They look like the soldier-fabers found in the woods," Chi replied.

So the plague had spread, Bao thought. It was killing villagers and soldier-fabers alike. Bao remembered the faces of the soldiers he had found. Their faber faces looked almost human. In death we all look the same, he thought, suddenly feeling dizzy. And this is a new death.

"What did you find in the headquarters hutch?"

"Only fabers," Chi said. "Dead. No men."

"Is the cache cellar locked?" Bao asked.

"Yes."

Bao would have to go into the village, for the heavy steel doorslide of the cache cellar was only keyed to soldier-missionaries. Neither fabers nor *moi*-missionaries could gain entrance. But Bao would find supplies and safety in the comfortable bunker. And he could use the laser transceiver to call command post for new orders.

Before he could stand up, the nausea returned. He coughed and vomited a thin yellowish bile. He would rest a moment. His strength would return. But he was caught in a dream. He fought it. Old memories woke and left their dark places. Bao shouted. He was in a cold sweat.

And then he remembered that base *hai* had once been his home. He could not go back there, he told himself. Everyone he had known—the children he had grown up with, his teachers, Giay, the old men, the women—would be ghosts or spirits or strangers who thought the same thoughts, believed in the same divine cycle, and lived in the same dream.

He tried to shut out his memories, for he belonged to the state. He should not have memories, for the state had replaced them with *ching*-games and life-dreams and noble thoughts. Nevertheless, he remembered. Now he had a past. But he was lost. His memories were tearing him from the sacred web of state, the one true authority that presided over the earth and maintained the precarious balance of *ying* and *yang*.

Bao tried to forget his past which had formed like frost on cold metal. But it was too late. Memories crawled out of the filthy caverns and stinking closets of his mind. He stood up and directed his fabers to fan out around him. Then he began walking toward his village. He imagined that he was already dead.

He was finally going home.

Bao entered the village from the east. He followed a muddy path around hutches which were in various states of disrepair. In this climate the crude huts had to be mended daily. Village life was a constant battle against wind, rain, *moi*, and the ever encroaching jungle of flatfronds, saucerleaf, silverglitter, and crawlervine. Beyond the hutches was the silvery *dinh*—the village longhouse, and beyond that was the pebble garden which contained the eternal spirits of the village.

As Bao approached the *dinh*, he was overwhelmed by the stench of putrefaction. Villagers were sitting and praying inside a circle of dead bodies. Women, children, old men and fabers had been laid out to form a mandala of flesh. The human corpses were black and blue; they looked as if they had been beaten. Their bellies were distended, and their bloated bodies were covered with large sores. The few fabers that were laid out on the outside edge of the mandala were also swollen and discolored. Their scale-plates had fallen away to reveal sores and mottled grey flesh. Effigy-dolls hung from high poles which were positioned north, south, west, and east of the mandala. They represented the four keepers of death.

"What are you doing there?" Bao asked the villagers who stared past him, as if looking into private worlds or watching invisible spirits swimming in the clear air.

No one answered him. Even the children seemed to be lost in the magic of the mandala. But Bao remembered something Giay had said to him long ago: "What you see with your eyes is not always real. Your mind can see much more clearly." Then Bao understood that the mandala of the dead was made to keep out *ma quy*. The villagers could only see their village spirits. They were blind to anything outside the mandala.

Keeping a good distance away from the villagers, he walked over to headquarters hutch, which had been scorched and structurally damaged. The villagers probably did it, he told himself. They would blame the plague on *outsiders*. He could almost visualize the brown mud and sarissa hutch as a great wounded animal hunched over on its forepaws. He stepped over the bits and pieces that had once been a porch. Chi was waiting for him in the doorway.

"Three faber-soldiers were found inside," Chi said, as he helped Bao into the hutch. Bao felt weak and sweaty again. He sat down in a worn wooden chair.

"Where are they now?" Bao asked, looking around the room. Then he looked outside at the faber-soldiers regrouping in front of the hutch. They huddled close together, as if to keep warm.

"They were taken behind the third hutch."

"Bury them," Bao said as he activated the doorslide to the cellar cache. As the door slid open and the bunker lights blinked on, he heard a woman's voice speaking in a soft monotone.

". . . remain calm . . . an antidote has been found . . . remain at your posts . . . help will arrive . . . shortly . . . in the meantime . . . keep your distance from anyone . . . faber or human being . . . who . . . the symptoms of the virus are . . . corpses must be burned immediately . . . attention . . ."

Bao climbed into the bunker and switched off the laser transceiver. The room stank. A missionary was slumped over the small workbench beside the transceiver. Bao did not touch him, as he could see the sores on the man's hand. He called Chi, told the faber to have the dead man taken outside where he would be burned. Then Bao checked the storeroom, which was little more than a closet. Although most of the food and medical supplies had been removed, Bao was grateful for the few ration packs and food cannisters that he found.

The men must have used the tunnel, he thought, resting his hand on the metal handle of the tunnel-hatch. The tunnel was a narrow passageway, barely wide enough for a man to crawl through, which opened behind a copse of redknob outside the village.

Just as he was about to leave the bunker, Bao experienced a slight delirium. And he felt something growing inside him, something alive and slippery, something with tiny claws at the end of thinsmooth feelers. He fell, and the room seemed to be whirling around him. His fingers scrabbled about on the floor like live things searching for darkness and cool safety.

When he awakened, he found that he was drenched in his own sweat. He shivered, made a resolve to fight his weakness, and crawled out of the bunker.

"All the corpses must be burned," he said to Chi, who had been waiting in the hutch for further orders. Then Bao stepped out of the hutch into the bright sunshine. He took a deep breath of fresh air, and imagined he was breathing the effluviums of death.

Before him, just beyond the pebble garden, the villagers sat inside their mandala, their backs facing outward. They chanted the prayers of exorcism. Bao walked to the edge of the garden and shouted to them. But they ignored him. He was only *moi.*

Bao signalled to Chi, and the fabers moved in to carry away the corpses. A pyre of sarissa and softwood had been prepared behind the hutches, well away from the village center. The corpses would have to be burned immediately.

But the villagers would not permit their mandala to be disturbed. They snarled and shouted and prayed. They pummelled and kicked the faber-soldiers, called them death-*moi,* shouted at Bao, told him to take away his demons, for he was *ma quy,* and he would never find his way into their souls. They would hold their breaths if he came near; they would not breathe his death-fumes.

Bao understood their threats. He felt like a ghost or a demon, a maleficent spirit that had somehow escaped from the darkness of the caves of hell. He fired a warning shot over the villagers. They became silent and turned away from him. The soldiers quickly removed the corpses to the pyre which had just been set afire.

As Bao watched the corpses blacken in the flames, he remembered events and emotions of his childhood. He imagined that his past was just another corpse burning in the fire. His memories were streamers of black smoke drifting skyward.

But they would return, he thought, as the black rain of his dreams.

The *moi*-attack came with dusk. The new offensive had begun. It was as if the grey-turning-into-darkness had brought all the noise and shadow-figures and pinch-bombs. Hutches exploded. Villagers were shot as they ran toward the *dinh* or into the fields which had been set aflame. *Moi*-fabers rushed into the village. They tripped mines, died in trapwire and automatic crossfire. But still they came. It was as if they had been spawned from dragons' teeth. For every *moi*-faber that fell, there would be another to replace him. Everything was soon covered in smokeover mist. The crackcrack of rifles and the yellow flares of small bombs became the thunder and lightning of a deadly storm.

Bao knew that he could not hold against this attack. Although his fabers still held their positions and slaughtered *moi* in a carefully planned crossfire, they would soon be overwhelmed by sheer numbers of *moi*-soldiers. Somewhere in the hills, Bao told himself, there was a missionary directing this attack and watching the smoke and fire from a safe distance, as if he was playing a *ching*-game that would come out right in the end.

But Bao was sick. He vomited every few minutes. The yellowish bile stank, and he imagined that he was rotting from the insides. Still, he tried to make his way to headquarters hutch. His only chance was the tunnel, he told himself as he took cover and rested for a moment behind a hutch. The hutch burst into flames. The heat was a wave pushing outward, overtaking him, wafting over him. He rolled away and screamed. His past had overtaken him.

Chi pulled him behind another hutch. Bao could hardly see in the smokeover. He hoped *moi* would shoot him. He imagined that ghosts were drifting through the smoke.

"Stay here," Giay said. He had become just another smoke-ghost. *"If you leave, your soul will remain behind with the bones of your ancestors. You'll destroy your past and future. You'll have nothing left but an eternal present."*

"This is your home," his mother said as she drifted in the flames.

Bao cried as an explosion changed the pressure in his ears. He could hear only a constant roaring. Something knocked him over, and he was lost in darkness. He dreamed that the world was slowing down, unwinding, dying.

He dreamed that he was dead.

When he awoke, he felt Chi's dead weight on top of him. He pushed himself away from the faber and crawled through the roiling smoke to die alone. He laughed and imagined that he was a smoke-ghost. *Moi* could not find him, he thought. He dreamed that he was crawling with Chi. He had only the present, the dead comfort of *now*. Each *now* was a dream, an empty space. *Ying. Yang.*

Bao had made it out of the smoke and fire. He rested near a copse of sleeping willows and Christmas memory. Below him, past sarissa and paddies aglow with rootstalk, the village was buried in smokeover.

It didn't matter if he was caught now, he told himself. His diseased spirit would escape through his mouth to deliver death to the enemy. He would be a tool of the state. But Bao did not care: It could be *ying* or *yang,* love or hate, the wheel would still turn. Perhaps not, he thought. Then the divine cycle would be broken. He felt the gentle touch of childhood memories.

Above him, above the ticktick rattling of rifles, the sparkling fragments of the ring were moving imperceptibly across the clear night sky. It was as if the hidden fires of the village were reflected in the heavens, Bao thought. He remembered the legend of Tan Ming Hoang, the ruler of the world who was trapped in the sky.

A flare burst beyond the mountains. It was a white flower of pure daylight. Shadows lengthened, then faded back into the soft depths of night. Bao listened for the barking of rifles, but heard only familiar nightsounds.

He awoke, as if from a dream of grace, when he saw the ocean of red light behind his closed eyelids. He sat up and watched the red flowers blooming on the western horizon beyond purple mountains. The sky was like dark water, and a red dye was leaking, taking over the night with bleeding arms. As Bao watched the distant fires, he understood that the cycle had been broken. The ring could barely be seen in the sky. Surely Tan Ming Hoang could make his way back to earth now.

This was the time to leave, he thought, trying to die. But he could not push himself into death so easily. He stared into the bright night and waited, knowing that beyond his land a greater war had begun . . .

3298 A.D.

The flowing characters of history turn blood red. Casca and a few small states drag Dardania and Pindaria into a war involving biological as well as nuclear weapons, a conflict which ends in holocaust.

The only fortunate aspect in the use of atomics in those final days was that targeting was confined to a few large cities and to preemptive strikes against military bases . . .

. . . but the plagues engineered by biologists made little distinction between fabers and humans . . .

A terrible silence descends on Cleopatra . . .

—Hela Fenn, Psycho-Soc,
Colonial Survey, 3300 A.D.

WAYSIDE WORLD

by George Zebrowski

The city sat in the hill, rising upward from deep within the mass of earth, rock and vegetation to tower a kilometer into the night sky, its angled windows dark, reflecting only the bright stars and the faint rainbow of the ring; ten thousand windows, centuries old and unbroken, staring westward across the valley. Meteors flashed in the plastic panes, mute fireworks showing in black, sightless eyes long past celebration. The structure was an empty shell which had once housed a million people. A few still used it because the windows caught the sunlight, warming the outer layer of dwelling spaces through trapped heat.

At the edge of the world a morning storm flickered in the clouds which hid the dawnlight. The city's clear panels became blinking eyes, the sudden brightness of lightning destroying the mirrored ebony surfaces which held the cold starlight and dying meteor trails.

In rooms a third of the way up from the vegetation of the hillside, six people slept, derelicts in need of a dawn to stir them from their troubled sleep . . .

I

He opened his eyes suddenly and saw the light flashing through the windows, flooding the world with a blue-white wash. In a moment the drops were beating against the windows, running like tears down the inclines. The rain would make things grow; summer would last just a little longer. Sadness welled up within him. He started to repeat his name in the way his mother had once spoken it.

Call him Ishbok, his father had said a long time ago, but his mother had made it sound special. *Ishbok,* he whispered softly to himself, trying to catch the musical quality of his mother's voice.

The others did not waken, and the storm seemed to rage over their stillness. The water washed downward in a river; the thunder walked with the footsteps of a giant. The full force of the storm rode over the valley, holding back the light of sunrise.

Ishbok looked around at his sleeping companions, at Foler, who also wanted Anneka; at Foler's younger brother, Thessan, who would never be well; at Anneka sleeping next to her dying parents. The old couple were fading fast, sleeping away most of each day; there was nothing to be done except make them comfortable and bring them what little food they were able to eat. *Why could we not have been trees,* Ishbok thought, *or the stones which seem able to keep their pride. We are soft and filled with blood, and a dried sarissa bamboo point is enough to kill us . . .*

Foler already spoke as if Anneka belonged to him. His every glance was a challenge. Ishbok was avoiding a fight, hoping that Anneka would say how she felt. Sometimes he felt shamed and angry at her silence. He did not want to fight Foler, even if a fair fight were possible; Thessan would join in like a stupid dog defending his master. The dark-haired older brother's friendly smile hid the truth—he was always ready to let things happen, as long as it served his wants.

After Anneka's mother and father died, Foler would take the daughter. If Ishbok tried to stop it, he would die; if he did nothing, he would live. It was as simple as that. *He's afraid to take her while the old live,* Ishbok thought. *He's afraid of their curses. He fears unseen things more than me. He controls Thessan with his own fears . . .*

For a moment Ishbok imagined what it would be like to be Thessan. Without Foler, nothing was certain. Foler knew where all the food was to be hunted or found; he kept evil things away at night. Foler had to be obeyed; there was no other way. Foler made him feel good; Foler made him feel safe.

Thessan was like a faber, except fabers were much more alert; fabers had pride. Ishbok felt sorry for Thessan; but being sorry would not help him, as hatred would not make his brother better.

Across the room Foler stirred and sat up while prodding Thessan awake. His eyes were watchful, suspicious; but in a moment his gaze became uncaring as he realized that Ishbok would not have waited for wakefulness to kill him. Slowly Foler got to his feet. *He knows I couldn't do it, he's sure of it.*

"Coward!" Foler threw the word like a stone.

Anneka woke up, pulling the blanket around her for protection. She sat up and looked at Ishbok. He thought he saw reproach in her expression, but the light was too faint to be sure. There would be no smile or look of sympathy, only the look of resignation. *Anneka... Anneka,* he said silently, *I made none of this, but I love you.*

"Unwind your stringy muscles," Foler said to him, "we have food to find."

The thunder exploded again and water ran in noisy rivulets on the windows. Foler's face was a grinning skull with caves for eyes.

Anneka began to braid her long brown hair, her eyes cast downward. She looked up only to glance at the storm outside.

Ishbok watched her from where he sat on his blanket. His stomach was cold and empty. He shivered, thinking of the warm sun; it would make food-searching a little easier.

Anneka's father woke up, breathing badly and coughing.

"The old fool should be dead," Foler said stretching. Then he held out a hand and helped Thessan stand up.

Anneka's mother woke up, wailing about her blindness.

"Keep her quiet," Foler said. Ishbok saw a fearful

look take hold of Foler's face. "They should both be dead."

"They'll die, they'll die," Thessan chanted, hoping to please his brother. Foler grinned and patted him on the back.

Suddenly Thessan lumbered across the large room to a window and placed his large palms against the moisture-laden interior surface. He washed his face, chuckling to himself.

"It's a dark rainy morning," Anneka said to her mother, stroking her forehead. Her husband reached over and held her bony hand. The old woman subsided into a soft throat clearing.

Foler went over to the window and slapped some moisture on his face. Ishbok stumbled to his feet and walked over to a fresh window. He cupped some wetness and put it to his face.

Foler laughed. "Not much hair to wash on him."

Ishbok looked up to see Thessan standing next to him, grinning and running his fingers through his dirty beard.

Ishbok turned away from him and took a few steps toward the door.

Anneka tied her braids off with two bits of leather and stood up. "I'm ready," she said.

Foler went past Ishbok and turned in the door. "A strong woman—not for you. With that soft hide of yours, you'd bleed to death from her scratches."

Ishbok felt the anger swell in himself, but he looked away from Foler's eyes.

"You're not worth killing," Foler continued. "One day you'll break your own neck and save me the trouble. You're good for picking roots, berries and nuts. Even Anneka can kill an animal for food." He paused. "Ah, let's get going!" He turned and went out into the hall and toward the stairs. Ishbok followed, thinking suddenly that he might run up behind Foler and push him to his death; but in the next moment he was flat on his face as Thessan pulled his feet out from behind. Ishbok's jaw hurt from the impact. Thessan stumbled across him and ran after his brother, laughing.

Anneka helped him to his feet and walked toward the stairs without a word. Slowly Ishbok followed, feeling no hatred now, only shame and sadness, the coldness in his stomach a heavy weight slowing his steps.

Foler led them upstream through the center of the valley. Thessan followed close behind him. Anneka walked a dozen paces behind Thessan. Ishbok was last.

The clouds of morning passed. Anneka's hair turned a bright red in the sun rising at their back. Ishbok walked slowly, watching her. Despite her clothing from the oldtime, the patched trousers, leather belt, sweater and boots, she seemed gentle marching across the mossy turf next to the stream.

Morning mists rose from the valley as the sun warmed the earth. The silence of his own breathing and the steadiness of the stream at his right calmed him. Far ahead to his left the red-coned evergreens sat on the mountainside; around them nestled sugarroot bushes, their leaves and pulpy twigs laden with the sweetness of late summer.

Slowly Foler was making a circle which would lead them up into the hills. They would eat the sugarroot, and then there would be enough strength to bring down some game and carry it home. Ishbok licked his lips at the thought of the sugarroot.

Maybe today they would bring down a hipposaur when it came to drink the stream water and graze on the green moss; maybe today luck would give them enough food for a week's rest in the city.

But quickly he remembered that full stomachs and rested muscles would help them forget the need they all had of one another. Foler would want Anneka again; Thessan would be bored and hard to control.

A jumpingtom raced across Foler's path. Foler raised

his boomerang and let fly, cursing as it missed. He went to get it back. Ishbok heard more cursing.

"Ishbok, come here!" Foler shouted.

Ishbok hurried.

"It broke on the stone—you'll have to make a new one. Better make two." Foler was almost friendly.

If I make too many spares, Ishbok thought, *you won't need me.* "I can only work so fast," he said softly, "and not at all when I'm hungry and afraid."

Foler's dark eyes were scornful. His eyebrows went up and he grinned through his beard. "I'm the best thrower."

Anneka could do it.

Foler turned away and continued on the path to the sugarroots. Ishbok followed. Thessan came up behind him and pushed him out of the way to get back near his brother. Ishbok turned his head to see Anneka walking steadily behind him. She did not look up and he turned away to fix his gaze on the red cones ahead.

As he walked he thought of the stories about the old sicknesses, the war plagues, the fireballs that left heaps of dead, the skeletons in the cities. He had never seen any of these things, but his mother's vivid tellings lived in his mind. He remembered his father's look of reproach when he would find her giving such life to the past.

Those who lived had found each other among the dead, in cities which stood unharmed, yet were gutted. The survivors knew the value of human life, acting out of necessity, clinging to each other in resignation and acceptance. So it had been for more than two generations. Ishbok's father and mother had met in the great empty city by the northern lake. From there they had travelled down to the southern ocean, in time for Ishbok to be born in a small stone house near the water. His father had complained that there were few old-time libraries in the smaller southern cities, and that Ishbok would not survive as well in a colder climate as if he were born in a warmer place.

But life will be easier here, his mother had said, *and we don't have to go back.*

He'll have to go back to learn, his father had answered.

When he is older, he'll go back well enough . . .

One day dark men had come out of the swamp to spear his father to a gnarly dwarf tree and carry his mother away like a four-footed animal hanging from a stick, her long black hair dragging on the ground . . .

Ishbok remembered the sick feeling in his stomach as he had been picked up and hurled down from a cliff into the sea. But his small body had missed the rocks. His cheek touched bottom gently and he pushed himself upward with his hands. He swam as he had been taught and the waves washed him ashore with only a few cuts from the rocks. He remembered his own blood on the sand when he had gotten up hours later, his tears burned away by the hot sun.

The little house was empty when he returned. In the silence of sea and memory he heard again his father's wish that he should learn about the world before life came to an end. When he looked at the body pinned to the tree, he imagined that his father's life had become joined to the twisted trunk, his flesh drinking now the moisture brought up by the tree's deeply searching roots.

Traveling north, he had searched for the libraries which held the books he knew how to read. He could not read all the languages brought to Cleopatra by the colonists from Earth, but he could always understand his own, and much of two others. The libraries spoke about one another, sending him amongst themselves as would jealous guardians who share a favorite child. The old buildings gave him shelter and knowledge—the knowledge of stored foods and where to find them. In winter the food enabled him to stay in one place as he studied. Once he had been forced to burn a few of the books he could not read to keep warm, telling himself that he would never find anyone who could tell him what they were about. Besides, the books spoke of other kinds of books, known things stored in machines which gave knowledge for the asking; he was sure there was more than one copy of the volumes he had burned.

In the empty cities he had come upon small bands of men and women. Sometimes they would accept him, with suspicion; he would stay for a time, to leave or to be driven off sooner or later.

He had come into Anneka's group five summers ago. Her parents could still walk then. Foler and Thessan had been friendly, especially after finding out he could make knives, spear points and boomerangs—and keep the weapons sharper than they had ever known. But no matter how long Foler watched him work the old metal on the stream stones, he could not match Ishbok's skill. One day Thessan had tried sharpening to please his brother. Foler had beaten him for ruining two knives, but Ishbok had saved the edges.

So little of what he had learned in the libraries could be turned into useful things. Knowledge had made him feel pity, and the need for another kind of learning, barely glimpsed, one which might again create the realities of the old time.

Ishbok turned to look back at the city, set like a blue gem in the mossy mountain, entranceways hidden in foliage. The towering place was always a reminder of exile from a better past. The structure soared upward, a relic of powers he could not summon; the sight gave him hope, at the same time making him feel small. He felt anger in his humiliation, and turned quickly to follow Foler and Thessan before Anneka caught up to him.

Foler and Thessan were on their knees eating leaves from the sugarroot bushes. Ishbok sat down under a red-coned evergreen and picked a leaf from the nearest bush. Anneka was only a few paces behind him. She came up past him and sat down near the brothers without looking at him.

Ishbok swallowed the sweet juice and spit out the pulp. His stomach rumbled.

"Fabers!" Foler whispered loudly.

They all stood up and turned to look where he was pointing. On the angle of the mountainside, shapes stood among the evergreens, scaly manlike forms with long necks and slender tails.

Receding clouds let sunlight fall between the trees, scattering patches of bluish yellow on mossy rocks and soft earth. Somewhere a tree spook cried out and was still, reminding Ishbok of the colorfully plumed jackdandies he had known as a child. In the silence of sun and shadow, the fabers began to move, stepping softly, surely, as if the evergreens had sprouted legs.

As the saurians moved in and out of sunlight, Ishbok saw the v-shaped mouths of the closest ones, set in the familiar grin; the golden eyes were wide under ridges, the skullcap crests suggesting the helmets of old time warriors from other times, other worlds.

But these fabers would not fight; they moved too slowly. These were not like the changed ones who had once fought for men. These were the dying ones, easy to kill and eat, yet they seemed to mock their destroyers.

Foler loosed his remaining good boomerang. It flew between the trees like a diving cinnamon bat and felled the forward faber. The creature tumbled down the incline while its companions stopped and switched their tails in agitation.

"Better than pig," Thessan said as he stopped the body's roll with his foot.

"We can cut it up and go home," Foler said.

Ishbok watched the single slit nostril of the dying faber as it drew in air in hungry rasps. The mouth was open, revealing the nearly human teeth set in a delicate jaw.

Thessan picked up a large rock and caved in the skull. When he stepped back the golden eyes were closed. The claw-tipped hands unclenched.

Ishbok looked up the mountainside, but the rest of the fabers were gone, leaving a mournful silence for the one who had died.

"Lucky it was not a killer pack," Foler said. He knelt down with Anneka and his brother. Together they began to cut up the body with their knives, selecting the best portions.

"We'll cut some hide to carry the meat in," Foler said.

Ishbok's stomach rumbled again, loudly enough to be heard. Foler laughed at the sound and continued cutting.

My knives, Ishbok thought. For Anneka the flesh meant a few days of life for her parents, and a more comfortable dying. Ishbok turned away as Thessan started to chew a piece of uncooked flesh.

"Here," Foler said. Ishbok turned to receive a wrapped cut of meat. "You carry one if you want to eat." *For Anneka's sake,* he told himself. "One day we'll find their eggs," Foler added.

A wind came up as the sun neared noon. It rushed through the trees like an angry thing. Red cones fell as if they were solid drops of blood. Ishbok thought that at any moment the wind would cry out in a shriek above its own fearful whispering.

As they marched back toward the city, Ishbok knew that he would eat the faber's meat with the others. His portion was not very heavy, but they were all weak from the morning's march; the meat held them together with its promise of rest. He would eat the meat as long as it was cooked, however badly.

Across the valley the city was a mirrored sheet of golden sunlight set against the hills, rising upward to a spear point in a blue sky. Ishbok wondered as he walked behind Foler and Thessan and Anneka. He tried to imagine all the things that he would never know —the skills which enabled men to live longer, heal their wounds, reach beyond the world.

He remembered reading about the giant city which sat on Charmian, moon-sister of the world; beings like himself had made a place for themselves there also. Others had traveled through the space between worlds, perhaps even to other stars.

Behind the city's spear point there was a large flat place where flying machines had once come to land, leaving off travellers and picking up new ones. He had seen a picture in a book. Long ago he had promised himself that he would climb up there, if he ever found the city. From that place, he had imagined, he would see more than anyone had seen in a long time.

Ishbok lay on his blankets in the corner of the room. Thessan was urinating on the small fire near the open window. The smell of burnt meat was still strong, despite the cool evening air drafting from the window through the door into the corridor. Anneka was with her parents, speaking softly to them. Foler lay on his blankets in the corner opposite from Ishbok. Anneka's parents had not been able to eat much. Half of the carcass was still uncooked.

"Fire's out," Thessan said.

The shadows of sunset seemed almost purple; the windows were panels of airy blue. Ishbok closed his eyes and saw the faber's face in the moment before the wise golden eyes had closed.

"Fire's out," Thessan repeated.

"Go to sleep," Foler said.

In time, Ishbok told himself, Anneka would belong completely to Foler and his brother. He saw himself moving on to another place, another group. If Anneka became heavy with Foler's child, that would be enough.

Foler would lose an edgemaker; Ishbok would lose Anneka. *I have no courage,* he said to himself.

Ishbok opened his eyes and saw stars twinkling brightly in a darkening sky. His eyes were heavy. He felt uncaring in the tired satisfaction of his full stomach. Thessan had gone to lie down next to his brother. They were sleeping beasts and could not harm him. Faber faces mocked him when his eyes closed; yet their expressions also seemed pitying. A dark tide came in upon him, billowing clouds of darkness carrying him away from all awareness.

II

Anneka's sobbing woke him near dawn. He lifted his head and saw her kneeling over her parents, a dark form against the pale light coming in through the windows.

He raised himself and crawled toward her, until he could see the old couple lying together in death. He got up on his knees and was still. Anneka did not look at him as she hovered over the lumpy masses of the dead.

Thessan began to snore loudly.

Ishbok knew that the old ones could not have lived much longer. Both had been more than thirty years old, though he had read that in the old time people had lived to a hundred. Even so the feeling of uselessness had contributed to their death.

In the corner beyond, Foler woke up to watch. Thessan began to snore even more loudly than before. Foler poked him in the ribs and the snoring stopped.

Anneka lay down next to her parents as if to imitate their stillness. In his corner Foler lay back and went to sleep. Ishbok moved backward on his knees and crawled under his blankets.

After a while sleep returned. Gratefully, he drifted away from the presence of death.

He awoke after what seemed a very long time, but the pale light of dawn was not much brighter than before. He sat up and looked around the room. Anneka was not with her parents. He peered across the room and saw her bare shoulders next to Foler's.

Ishbok got up on all fours and started to crawl toward her, his heart a cold stone in his chest. In a moment he saw that her dark eyes were open wide, staring at the ceiling as she clutched her portion of the gray blanket.

A whistle of air escaped from Thessan, who now slept a dozen paces away, like a dog who has been driven away for the night.

Ishbok stopped crawling. Anneka turned her head and looked at him, staring at him as if from out of a dark cave.

"Get away!" she whispered, baring her teeth grotesquely.

"Anneka . . ."

Foler awoke suddenly, saw him, and laughed.

"Swine," Ishbok said softly.

Foler propped himself up on one elbow and regarded him with mock seriousness. "If you weren't so useful I would kill you. Maybe I'd let Thessan do it."

"Go away," Anneka said. "Don't fight with him."

Ishbok stood up and said, "I'm leaving this morning."

Foler looked uncertain as he stood up wearing only his pants and boots.

Ishbok felt all his muscles tense as the thought of having been wrong about Anneka took hold of him. What did she see in Foler, who would lend her to his brother as easily as he would spit. He looked into her eyes, but they still stared at him from beyond the shadows.

Thessan awoke and giggled.

"You're not going to leave," Foler said. "I'll beat you into death first."

Anneka turned her face away from him.

"Filthy swine," Ishbok said, "you're no better than an animal."

Foler lunged at him, but Ishbok stepped to one side, turned and ran out the door into the corridor. Behind him Thessan was shrieking with glee.

Without stopping, Ishbok started to climb the stairway. He went up three stories without stopping.

His heart was pounding wildly when he stopped to listen. An acid taste had come up from his stomach. He threw up a little onto the black finished floor of the landing. He staggered toward the door which led into the city level and looked inside. Dark. He could not see inside.

Suddenly he heard a noise from below. Foler and Thessan were coming up after him. He turned in time to see Foler reach the landing, knife in hand.

Ishbok ran into the darkness of the room. As his eyes adjusted, he saw a door ahead of him, outlined in pale light. When he reached it a dark figure stepped into the frame. Ishbok heard Thessan's idiot laugh echo in the empty room. Somehow Thessan had reached this level by another way. The brothers were playing with him, he realized. He stopped and heard Foler come through the door behind him.

The thought of being beaten by Foler and Thessan was suddenly unbearable. Ishbok rushed toward Thessan's dark form. He bent low and knocked the shadow on its back with his head. The impact sent both of them sliding on the black floor until they came to a stop in the center of the next room.

Here the windows were gray with dawnlight. Ishbok saw another door at the far end as he scrambled to his feet. Thessan was clutching at him and shrieking. Ishbok kicked him in the ribs to free his right foot, and raced across the polished floor, out into the corridor and up the stairs. He heard Foler screaming at Thessan as he climbed, but when he paused on the next landing he heard only his own breathing.

"When I catch you," Foler shouted suddenly, "you'll never lech after a woman again!" His laugh echoed in the stair space.

Ishbok's one hope was to outlast the brothers in the climb. If he could get enough of a lead, then he could hide on one of the levels. They would not be able to guess where he had left the stairs.

He went up two more levels and stopped. Heavy footsteps chattered like curses from below. He took another deep breath and fled up the stairs, trying to step as lightly as possible.

One stretch of stairs, then another; a landing, the next stretch, a new landing, and the next. His bare feet were being burned by the friction of leather in his boots. After half a dozen turns he began to feel pain in his lungs. His heart was going to burst and his eyes would pop out of their sockets; he forced himself to the next landing and stopped.

He filled his lungs with air and held his breath for a few seconds, but the pulse of blood in his ears drowned all sound from below.

Gradually he heard the wheezing and labored breathing of the two men. Foler's curses grew louder, threatening to erupt as visible monstrosities; Thessan's high-pitched shrieks were snakes constricting the physical deformities conjured up in Ishbok's mind by Foler's wrath.

Foler's head appeared as he turned to climb the final stretch of stairs. Ishbok turned to climb higher and slipped on the polished surface before the first step. His forehead hit the fourth stair. He lay stunned, clawing at the railing.

In a moment the brothers were on him, collapsing on

top of him in a heap. Foler was cackling. "Hold him down, Thes, then I'll cut it off and throw it down—"

Ishbok punched him in the face, and with a lucky thrust put a finger in Thessan's eye. Then he stood up, picking up the knife Foler had dropped.

As he went up the stairs, Ishbok dropped the knife down the stairwell. He reached the next landing and ran into the empty room. The one beyond it was bright with the orange light of the sun rising through the morning storm clouds. Ishbok passed into a third room. Here the windows were being dotted with the first rain drops of the storm. At the other end of the room he went through a door and found more stairs.

He went down two levels and hid in a windowless chamber. He tried to relax in the dark corner. If they caught up with him again, he would need all his strength. His best hope was that they were now as tired as he was, and would not want to waste the day. There was no food in the upper levels of the city; either Ishbok would come back or starve. If he tried to leave the city, they would be waiting. An upward climb would help him only briefly. Even if he could sneak past them into the countryside, they would track him like an animal. And today they would have food; tomorrow they would have food, while he would be weaker.

After a long while he got up, deciding that he would rather starve and die than be captured for the amusement of Foler and Thessan. They would humiliate him in front of Anneka, maiming and disfiguring him permanently. Then he would never be able to leave the group. He would not be able to hunt. He would grow old exchanging his skills for food and protection. They would force him to teach Anneka's sons. And when he was old and useless and empty of dreams, they would turn him out to die.

Anneka had never loved him; he had proof enough of that. But before he died, he would reach the top of the city. That much he could still accomplish; he would keep faith with his wish of long ago.

He fled upward for most of the morning, stopping to rest in dozens of rooms. The rain stopped and the sun rose with him, looking into the windows, lighting up his way, warming the chill of morning. He would stop occasionally to hear the sound of air coming up the stairwell, the sound of a breathing beast about to be loosed after him. The sight of Anneka with Foler would not fade from behind his eyes. His muscles were tight as he climbed; his mind held a naked hope, almost as if there would be some kind of answer at the top of the city, something so much greater than his life that it would destroy the hurt of the morning. He willed himself upward.

Finally, he came through the opening which led him out onto the flat area behind the great spire. He felt like a wanderer in a dream state. His lungs were heavy, his feet hurt, and he felt dizzy. The sun was hot on his face. It had won the race toward noon. The air was still and hot. He stopped to wipe the sweat off his face with the sleeve of his hide jerkin.

Ahead lay an open plain of metal. On it sat more than thirty aircraft from the old time, huge metallic birds, motionless. He walked toward them slowly, forgetting for a moment the reality of loss behind him.

He stopped beside one of the flying things and pulled himself up inside through an opening. He was inside a bubble-like window. He imagined that the craft was moving through the clouds, carrying him away from the city, freeing him of his prison.

His whole life had been a confinement. He would not have Anneka. There would be no children to weep over his death. He might have told them his dreams. Now there would be nothing.

He looked up at the blue sky. It was a desert of false promises, beckoning him on with unreal suggestions of worlds beyond; there was nothing there that could help him.

As his strength drained away, he sat back in the bubble. The climb had taken all his energy. There was no way to gain it back. Sleep was the only escape.

He woke up choking on the hot air trapped inside the bubble. The afternoon sun was a blinding fire in the sky, rousing him back to the struggle of his life. Death and his brother, sleep, fled before the eye of Caesar as he scrambled out of the aircraft.

A strong breeze cooled him. Huge clouds sat on the northern horizon, promising a storm by evening.

He walked to the edge of the city and looked out over the countryside of green hills and rocky outcroppings and the blue stream which twisted away to the hazy blue at the end of the world.

He looked down and saw three people moving away from the city. The figures were so small, so insignificant; he felt no interest in them. And he felt no hunger or thirst. His warm body drank the cool wind. He shivered and turned to walk back toward the flying machine. Perhaps he could rest under a wing.

He opened his eyes at night and the infinity of sky and stars had become a cage. The ring was a barrier, saying to him that he had climbed so far and would be permitted to go no higher. This plain of metal would be his grave, guarded by mechanical birds. The wind would blow away his flesh, the sun would bleach his bones; starlight would enter the open eyes of his stony skull to stir whatever ghosts of thought remained. He would lie here forever, as dead as his world, scarcely more dead than the life into which he had been born. Caesar would burn away, the veil of air would be torn from Cleopatra, all the time of passing would dwindle, but he would never come again.

Ishbok closed his eyes, looking for a semblance of

peace within himself; now he found only weariness and hunger and hurt. He imagined the black wing of the aircraft moving down to cover him from the cold. Tears forced themselves out through his closed eyelids and he tasted their salt on his lips. The fever shivered his body.

Sleep came gently and he gave himself up to its calm.

III

Once, long ago, when he lay dying, a black dot appeared in the morning sky, growing larger as it came down until he screamed at its closeness. Then it crushed him and he had died.

Something strong held his head; his body was almost unfeeling. He opened his eyes. White, as if the very air were white. Black floaters in his eyes, flowing in and out of his direct vision. *Eye clouds,* his mother had called them, telling him to worry only if he saw one which did not move when he tried to look at it. Good food would always clear them up, and the same ones would not last more than a year.

He remembered light spilling out from an entranceway of some kind, like daylight but stronger, more like the white around him now. A strange thing sitting on the plain of metal . . .

Something was creating images in his brain, pushing him to think, changing him, prodding . . .

A man's garment reminded him of a mirror-wing moth, glittering. He sat in a small vessel, guiding it into a giant ship floating in the dark . . .

Time running backward . . . war fabers marching through snowy passes . . . across green fields . . .

An explosive burst of white light . . .

Plagues . . . piled bodies . . .

A world emptying out, subsiding into a terrible silence . . .

His world.

Reclaimed.

A word referring to him.

Others were being gathered from all over the world.

Slowly, thoughts became words, strange yet clear. Their meaning filled a need in him, one he had felt but never fully understood. Unfolding comprehension was wondrous, and frightening, as if the fiery sun itself were speaking to him.

". . . we have come to rebuild."

Suddenly he was rushing through space toward a yellow sun, and closer to linger over a blue world . . .

"Earth, the original home of your people and mine. The area of space within 500 light years of Sol is dotted with failed colonies established more than a thousand years ago. Most are lingering near death. Our newest ships will link these worlds into a loose confederation. We have brought tools, generating plants which have the power of small suns. We have synthesis techniques to help you make all that is needed for life."

Ishbok opened his eyes and saw the woman's face. "Why should you want to do all this?"

"We wish to help," she said. Her hair was white, clinging to her head in short curls; her eyes were green. "A confederation benefits all who belong. It is better to live under law, in social and physical health; a confederation is better than being alone."

Ishbok thought of the food-gathering groups he had known, and how they depended on each other, suffering from need and at each other's hands.

"But why talk with me?"

She smiled. "Because I think you understand, and that will help you lead your people."

"Lead?"

"Rest now. There will be more to learn later." Her

face receded into the white and a healing lethargy crept into his eyes, closing them.

He awoke feeling stronger than he had ever remembered; yet there was still a sense of struggle in his mind.

He knew so many new things, puzzling facts which he accepted without hesitation. The white room was in a giant starship circling Cleopatra. The starcrossing vessel was 10 kilometers long and capable of enormous velocities in excess of light speed. The offworlders had rebuilt his health. But he struggled with the thought of a device inside his head. "It will answer questions," the white haired woman had told him. Answers to any question he might think, as long as there was an answer in the starship's memory elements. He did not always understand the answers. There was a strange new country inside him, as vast as all the libraries he had known, as complete as all the knowledge of humankind, the central homefire of a species.

He tried to sit up and the bed shaped itself to support him.

It will always be a part of you now, the woman had said.

Who were these offworlders who could see inside each other? Was it right for anyone to have such power?

"We are your brothers and sisters." The words were inside him, whispering across the presence of knowledge which suddenly seemed a precious gift.

"But that is how you want me to see it!" Ishbok shouted and sat up in his bed.

A door opened in the wall to his left, startling him. The woman with white curls walked in and sat down in the chair next to his bed.

"You've been debating with your tutor-link quite a lot, sometimes even in your sleep." She smiled again. "Let's be friends, Ishbok. My name is Hela Fenn. You can call me Fenn. My profession is psycho-soc. Do you have another name?"

Ishbok noted that she had known his name, but he did not remember giving it to her. "It's the only one," he said, wondering how much of himself was no longer his own.

"How's your understanding of incoming material? Do you get a full picture of why we are here?"

Ishbok nodded. "How old are you, Fenn?"

"I'm forty."

Almost twice Anneka's age, older in earth years. Older than anyone he had ever known.

"Everything we've learned about you, Ishbok, indicates strong mental abilities in a number of directions. You understand alternatives quickly, you know how much you can do and not with the resources at hand; you will lead if given the chance, but you are willing to follow if you agree with one who leads—"

"How can you know these things? I don't even know them—"

"By your responses to dream strategies."

Ishbok felt a moment of fear.

"It's perfectly safe. Just like dreaming, except that certain decisive patterns are brought forward and reinforced."

"I don't like it and I don't want it ever again. And I don't know if I believe what you say about this tutor in my head. It seems to me that you may have the power to control my actions."

"Good," she said. "You're showing aggressively rational behavior. You'll need it to help your world."

He was about to object again, but he understood her.

"If you like," she said, "we can remove the link and give you an external head band—but that might be inconvenient. You might not have benefit when you most need it."

"Perhaps."

"Get dressed and we'll go to the observation deck.

Later we'll shuttle down to your city and get you started."

"You make it sound easy."

"Only the travel part, Ishbok," she said as she stood up. "The rest will be difficult, and you may fail." She turned and went out through the opening door, leaving him with a feeling of suspicion and apprehension.

Ishbok looked out into night and stars. Cleopatra glowed in blues and golds and browns, veiled in silvery clouds, encircled by the diamond dust of the ring, faceted debris and sculpted moons. Screens in back of him let in the light of Caesar; others showed space in various directions from the starship.

My world, he thought. *Nowhere is its suffering visible.*

"I'm sorry to be late," Hela Fenn said. He turned around as she was sitting down in one of the lounge chairs. She pointed to a seat opposite her own and put one foot up on the low table in the middle. "Sit down, Ishbok."

He noticed her clothes for the first time. One-piece green suit, wide pants, half boots. The garment came up around her neck in a tight fit.

"Do you really care?" he asked as he sat down.

"How do you mean?"

"My world—do you really care about helping?"

"I could give you a purely emotional answer which might please, but that would be to go against my convictions. Yes, we care, but we will all gain economically and socially. We are all Earth peoples. More than a thousand years ago, the home planet cast off its innovators, malcontents, idealists, dreamers — whatever name can be attached to them. A period of turmoil and cultural sterility followed, one which is not yet completely over. And this decline was mirrored in the history of every colony world we have visited. The colonists took bits and pieces of Earth with them, including all the old problems, and it shows in the state of every colony world we've seen.

"As nearly as we can make out from a year of investigation, the following is what happened on Cleopatra since the arrival of humankind more than a thousand years ago. A world grew in all directions from the place of landing. People grew different from one another; they moved away to create different places. The world filled up. Cleopatra changed. The local flora and fauna retreated before the life from Earth." She paused for a moment. "It's been coming back recently, but the world is a hybrid. Two kinds of fabers exist now, where once there was only one. At first fabers were modified to be workers and servants, and performers—dancers, musicians; they were also research animals. The warlike fabers hunt the original fabers, and men hunt them both.

"Anyway, the emerging nations grew apart. There were small wars and large wars; eventually a few small nations dragged Dardania and Pindaria, the largest powers, into a war involving biological weapons. It ended with a nuclear holocaust. The only good thing about the use of atomic weapons in those final days was that their use was confined to a few large cities and against military bases."

It's going to start all over, he thought, *unless we could become . . . something else, perhaps something that did not live on worlds where even simple things were lacking . . .*

". . . but enough has remained to start again."

"This ship is almost a small world, isn't it Fenn?"

"You can think of it that way. It's as large as many cities were in the past, in the centuries before space travel."

He looked directly at her for a moment.

"Is anything the matter, Ishbok?" Her look was helpful, serious, without guile.

"I'm wondering about what I have come to; if it is possible for me to be right."

"You're one of the ones Cleopatra needs." She spoke without a trace of hesitation.

"Why are you so sure—what do you know that I can't see?"

"I see what you will see when you find yourself in the reality of leading. You will know what to do, or you will not."

He stood up and turned away from her to look at the sight of Cleopatra. *They are all planning this,* he thought. *They think I will inevitably choose what they will agree with. What if I do things they cannot support? Surely they must know I am having doubts? Still, I cannot let the chance pass to stand between my people and these offworlders. I cannot let so much opportunity go by. She's right. I can help.*

He looked at the planet swimming in the starry void. *To them my world is an island.*

"I'll be with you to help, Ishbok," Hela Fenn said behind him. "I know what you must be feeling."

You may know too much, he thought. He wondered if they were capable of killing him; or if they were truly so wise as to know all the needs of his world, and his own.

He noticed then that she was standing next to him. There was a restrained pride in her stance, unlike anything he had ever seen in another person.

"If it will help you to know," she said, "there are those on Earth who oppose all the help we are trying to administer among the failing colonies. Our compromise with them is to let native leaders take the major role, whenever we can. To do nothing would be cruelty, don't you think?"

"I feel hopeful about what you say," he said, "but I must see more." *My world, my world, I pledge myself to you. I will do the best I know how, the best I can learn . . .*

"To be honest," she said, "there is some vanity in it."

Swirling clouds rushed up at the shuttle, replacing the sight of oceans and land with obscurity. *To come back and be so close,* he thought, *makes my world all the universe there is again.* He sat watching the forward screen in the passenger section of the shuttle. Hela Fenn sat next to him.

Soon the clouds broke and he saw the landing area of the city far below. The city grew larger.

"There will be a crowd," Hela Fenn said. "You know what to expect?"

"Yes."

"We're drifting down on gravs now. Try and smile when the crowd cheers. It's important to have them like you. Almost a quarter of all remaining human life has been gathered into this city since you've been gone. Do you feel the role you will play, my friend? Can you see your children and their future?"

He felt alone. "What will come must be better than what I grew up in." The crowd was looking up at him through the screen. The old air machines were gone, cleared by the off-worlders. He missed the old hulks.

The shadow of the circular shuttle grew smaller on the landing surface. The screen went dark as they touched, but went on again to show faces peering into the passenger section. Ishbok noted that they were mostly young faces—men and woman looking newly washed and fed, and cautious in their expressions.

Hela Fenn led the way out between the empty seats. Ishbok followed her to the center of the cabin. They stood together on the lift plate which dropped them down into the airlock.

The lock was already open, the oval exit framing the crowd outside. Hela stepped out first. Ishbok followed and stood next to her at the top of the ramp. The shuttle was a ceiling above them, casting a shadowy circle. Beyond the circle the crowd stood in Caesar's light.

Ishbok searched the faces of the closest ones, the unfamiliar faces filled with hope.

"One of your own!" Hela said, her voice booming from amplification and bouncing in the space under the shuttle. "He knows what Cleopatra needs; he knows what you need; he knows what the city needs. He will carry our help to you. Go to him, talk with him, tell him what can be done."

The crowd cheered. The sunlight seemed brighter.

"Soon the city's water, heat and light will be working fully. You will be able to farm the countryside; and later we will show you how to live without agriculture. These are material things only. Your task will be to educate yourselves, administer laws, reconciling all the differences between yourselves, the process which makes a state necessary." She stopped speaking. "Now, let's go down among them," she whispered.

Anneka's face caught him from the center of the crowd. He stood frozen, afraid, naked in his new clothes. Then he noticed Foler and Thessan standing next to her. *They don't recognize me,* he thought. Anneka seemed bewildered.

"We'll go through the crowd and down to your office and living quarters a floor below," Hela whispered. "You must go first."

Ishbok walked down the ramp, all the while staring at Anneka. When he reached the bottom of the ramp, he was too low to see her in the throng. Fenn was next to him. They walked forward.

The cheering resumed as the crowd parted for him. He walked ahead trying to smile as hands grasped at him and slapped his shoulders.

A man stepped in front of him. Ishbok recognized Foler—cleaner, shaved, dressed in offworlder fabrics, he was still surviving in his own way.

"What did you have to do to get all this, fool?"

You'll be opening a new period of history. The words chased each other through his brain. *Cleopatra will become a crossroads of interstellar commerce and cultural exchange.*

"You had better step aside," Hela Fenn said. "If this crowd hears you they'll tear you apart. Back off."

Foler stepped aside, his face mocking them. Ishbok hurried past him, through the rest of the crowd, and down a half-familiar flight of stairs. Hela Fenn was at his side as they came out into a lighted passage.

She walked ahead of him down the corridor, past one open door after another. Ishbok glimpsed workmen rebuilding the interiors. She stopped in front of a large door at the end. It slid open and he followed her inside.

"This is where you will live and work." The room was carpeted in soft green. A desk stood in the alcove of three windows, giving him an unobstructed view of the surrounding countryside.

"Come, sit down behind your desk," she said. She sat down in one of the chairs facing it. He sat down and looked at her.

"We're an empty world," he said, "which might be turned to advantages I can't guess yet."

"I picked you as one who would question and object," she said.

"On the way down you were telling me about history. Could you continue, Hela? I was very interested."

"I was talking about the need to break out of the cycles of prosperity and decline—the general rule among civilizations, at least the human ones we've seen."

"Are there others?"

"We don't know yet, but we're sure there are. Anyway, part of the answer lies in the use of vast resources, far beyond the kind available on a single planet. A single solar system is a good industrial base. The struggle then passes from a filling of material needs to a development of internal resources, the inner satisfactions of a human being. That part we don't fully understand yet. What we are fairly certain of is that there is no absolute necessity for the rise and decline of cultures. There may be a way out."

"What if you're wrong? What if it's always birth, decay, death, and new beginning. I see it in the man who stopped me outside, Foler."

"The new courts will deal with him."

"Can the courts take away his hatred of me? Can they remove his desire to mutilate me with a knife?"

Ishbok saw the pained expression on Hela's face. "I know you've seen a lot of darkness. But the light is there. We have to try."

Ishbok wondered if Anneka had gone to Foler out of choice, or to save the blademaker's life. Perhaps Foler had told her to play up to him so he would keep on producing tools; perhaps she even loved Foler.

"We're hoping that those like yourself, Ishbok, will have enough internal resources to resist decline."

"I cannot live forever. The time of those like Foler will come again." He smiled at her, feeling his own bitterness. "But I will try, Hela, I will try." *Anneka, did you save my life, even once?*

"Later . . . we'll send you a few security experts, Ishbok. They will help you train your own police force. There will also be experts who will help you run the city, including the schools, which will help create your own teams."

"Will my police carry weapons?"

"Harmless ones—the kind that can stop but not kill." She paused. "You will have enemies. The power will be yours to use. You will have to control it."

He saw Foler with a spear in his chest. Thessan hurtling to his death from the top of the city.

"I'm afraid of my thoughts, Hela, maybe you were wrong about me."

"If anything you convince me more. You're a kind,

concerned man, one who would never seek power; therefore you are the one who must use it. You will form a government and you will govern."

Suddenly the words ran out between them. *I can never be one of the offworlders,* his thoughts continued. *I've never belonged to any of the groups I've known. I've always been alone, holding back.* The awkward silence was a prison, an equilibrium of agreement and disagreement between Hela and himself. *And I am not completely a Cleopatran either.*

As if in answer, Hela Fenn said, "You will be the first of the new Cleopatrans. Let me tell you the story of Cincinnatus the Roman . . ."

IV

In the first months of mayorship, the representatives of the various groups gathering in the city came to talk with him; the captain of the starship paid a call, as did many volunteers from earth. The representatives confused him; the captain made him suspicious; the volunteers brought the skills he needed, so he put them to work. There were so many details in the doing of things that he almost forgot who he was.

"Leadership is being the center of a storm," Hela said in the second month. He was more interested in getting things done than in theorizing about them. There was more worry in thoughts than he could carry from day to day.

In the third month Foler raped one of the women volunteers from the starship, a medic. He held his own brother as a hostage to avoid capture by the police, and killed Thessan before surrendering. The trial which Ishbok had thought could be avoided was held. He did not attend and refused to have anything to do with it, although he might have been one of the three judges who heard the case.

"He grew up surviving," Hela had said to him. "He knows no other life and never will. His sense of inadequacy is complete in the new way of things, where nothing is open to him through the cruel means he knew in the past."

"I did not learn those ways."

"Your parents, Ishbok."

He sighed. "What will be the sentence?"

"We can retrain him, wipe memories, initiate new behavior and value patterns."

"You might just as well kill him—it's the same when you take away identity and memory."

"You could imprison him, or kill him instead. We'll do what we know how only with your permission, and if the court agrees."

"I don't know, Hela, I'll have to think." *Kill him! He's hopeless.*

"Let the courts decide," she said, "you're too close. If your courts don't have this power of decision, you'll have a world of power by individuals with no reference to laws."

The conversation had made him angry. The remembered rigmarole had not resulted in a solution for him. In a moment Anneka would come into his office. She was four months pregnant with Foler's child.

The door slid open. She came in and sat down in the chair in front of the desk. "I've come," she said, "to ask you not to kill Foler."

"I've made no plans to kill him, Anneka." *Anneka,* his thoughts whispered softly.

"And I want you to understand, more than anything," she continued without looking at him. "I chose him because I love him. But I would have chosen him anyway, because he was strong and would protect our children." She looked at him with tears in her eyes. "You are for another world. I tried to attract you so you would stay and make knives and points—I like you, but not as a lover or a father. I'm sorry, but don't kill him. I won't know what to say to his son."

"What if it's a daughter?"

"It will be a son," she said. A world of brutality stood behind her words, all of Foler's defiance and will, and she still lived in its service. *I could not be a father to her children,* Ishbok thought, *but I can be a protector of my city and my world.*

"He may not die, Anneka, but he may return . . . changed. It will not be my decision, but the court's."

She looked at him with doubt. "You let others make your choices—how can you be a man?"

"Don't you see, the same law must apply to all. I cannot decide. If I do, it will be meddling." *I'm not really sure,* he thought, *but I must decide.*

She stood up with restrained hatred in her eyes and spit at his desk.

She came to manipulate me again, he thought as Anneka turned and went out. The door slid shut and he sat in the silence of the room, listening to the sound of his pulse pounding in his ears, marking his own rising hatred, not only of Anneka and Foler, but of everything from which he had sprung.

The sooner it was swept away the better . . .

In the evening Ishbok was alone in the silence of the blood-red sun. He looked out across the valley at the deep blue shadows cast by the setting sun, and wondered about the future.

He tried to imagine this confederation, this greater world into which his wayside world would emerge. What battles, what disagreements would be possible there? What cycles of birth, decay and death, and new beginnings lay ahead for a civilization spanning the stars? How many isolate worlds were there tucked away in the miserable corners of the universe? He wondered if Cleopatra had better been left unfound, lost among the grains of stars, to rebuild by itself from its family squabbles rather than be shamed by intruders from the stars.

But he knew that it would be impossible now for him to see Cleopatra as the whole world; he had seen his home from beyond the sky, a glowing sphere set in a night of stars. He had seen its oceans, its land, the ring sweeping around the planet like unwanted riches being cast off into the void. He had looked down into the dark hemisphere where this city lay, invisible; he had seen it light up in the night, coming back to life after a thousand years.

Cleopatra circled Caesar, and Caesar was only one star among a countless number, yet all the importance of his life lay here. His own people would mistrust him, and he would mistrust the off-worlders; there was no safety in the thought. He would not be able to forget all that was; he would do his best to affect what would be.

Now he would have to be more than a warrior or a hunter or a craftsman, or a father; he would have to be a ruler, a helper.

The sun slid halfway behind the horizon. *I will have to learn to speak to my own people, as well as I speak with Hela. My children will have to know more than I do.* He thought of the many world histories belonging to the other worlds of the sky. He would ask Hela for them. Maybe there would be something he could learn from such a study. There were other reclaimed worlds entering the confederation. He tried to picture new, unspoiled worlds circling distant suns . . .

He thought of Anneka and her child. He wondered how the city would react to Foler's coming sentence, whatever that would be.

The sun was down. Stars appeared in the sky. Below him city light spilled out into the valley. The ring cut a swathe in the sky, a carpet preparing the way for chunky Charmian to rise and overtake Iras. Clouds sat on the northern horizon, promising a storm by morning. A black-winged deltasoar sailed into the twilight.

Ishbok stood up, sighing, knowing what he would do. He would govern with all the help there was to be had. He had become someone else, a stranger who would daily startle his earlier self; there was terror in the thought.

He knew that he would be lonely.

ABOUT THE AUTHORS

POUL ANDERSON is the author of over fifty books, including *Brain Wave, The High Crusade, Three Hearts and Three Lions,* and *Tau Zero.* His writing outside science fiction includes science fact, mystery, historical fiction, poetry, criticism, and translations. He has won five Hugo awards (given annually by the members of the World Science Fiction Conventions), two Nebula Awards (given each year by the members of the Science Fiction Writers of America), a Cock Robin Award for a mystery novel, and other honors. He is also a past president of the Science Fiction Writers of America. He lives in the San Francisco Bay Area with his wife, poet and writer Karen Anderson.

MICHAEL ORGILL is a freelance writer living in Glen Cove, New York. His short stories have appeared in a number of original collections, as well as in anthologies for young readers. He is the author of *Anchored In Love,* a biography of the Carter Family. At present he is working on an ambitious science fiction trilogy.

JACK DANN was born and raised in upstate New York. He studied drama at Hofstra University and received his B.A. in political science from the State University of New York at Binghamton (Harpur College). He studied law at St. John's University and did graduate work in comparative literature at S.U.N.Y. at Binghamton. His short fiction has been published in ORBIT, NEW DIMENSIONS, THE LAST DANGEROUS VISIONS, NEW WORLDS, IF, FANTASTIC, GALLERY, and other magazines and anthologies. He is the editor of WANDERING STARS, FASTER THAN LIGHT (with George Zebrowski), FUTURE POWER (with Gardner R. Dozois), THE SPECULATIVE FICTION YEARBOOK (with David Harris), and IMMORTAL. He is the author of a novel, STARHIKER. Mr. Dann is currently at work on a novel based on his novella *Junction,* which was a Nebula Award finalist. He has taught science fiction at Cornell University and Broome Community College. He was Managing Editor of the BULLETIN of the SCIENCE FICTION WRITERS of AMERICA from 1970 to 1974. Mr. Dann resides in Johnson City, New York.

GEORGE ZEBROWSKI is the author of more than thirty stories, articles and essays which have appeared in *Fantasy and Science Fiction, New Worlds, Amazing, Galaxy, If, Current Science* and other magazines, as well as in the many hardcover and paperback collections of original stories published since 1970. His novels include THE OMEGA POINT, STAR WEB, and MACROLIFE (forthcoming), a major novel on which he has spent most of a decade. He has been a Nebula Award Nominee in the short story. From 1970-1975 he was editor of the *Bulletin of the SFWA*. He is co-editor with Jack Dann of FASTER THAN LIGHT, HUMAN-MACHINES, with Thomas N. Scortia as well as the Planet Series of original collection from Unity Press in California. His interests include film, classical music, future studies, the philosophy of science, and chess. He lectures and has taught science fiction on the college level. Upcoming projects include a trilogy (of which THE OMEGA POINT is the central volume), and STAR WEB. He lives and works in upstate New York.